T0095469

The Amazing Adventures —*of*— JIMMY JUMPFERJOY

MARCUS BRUCE

authorHOUSE®

AuthorHouse™
1663 Liberty Drive
Bloomington, IN 47403
www.authorhouse.com
Phone: 1-800-839-8640

Published by AuthorHouse 11/21/2012

ISBN: 978-1-4772-8779-8 (sc)
ISBN: 978-1-4772-8778-1 (e)

Library of Congress Control Number: 2012920838

<u>DEDICATION</u>

This book is dedicated to my brothers
David and Keith Wright

Authors Note

When I was in high school my parents used to go out to dinner leaving me with my two younger brothers. They would often say tell us a story. So began the tales of Jimmy Jumpferjoy. I would ask them what kind of adventures he would have and they would tell me, it was interactive fun for all of us.

I took creative writing in high school and began to write down the stories. In college I took English Composition where I improved in my writing, and during a lonely year I spent on Martha's Vineyard without any friends, I began to step inside Jimmy Jumpferjoy's world. A two dimensional character became three dimensional.

I hope you have as much fun reading these stories as I had writing them!!!!!!!!!!

Contents

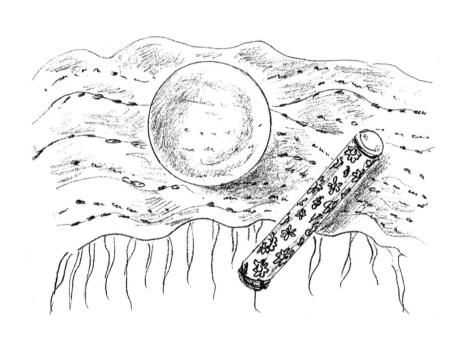

Chapter I

THE DISCOVERY

Jimmy was one of the friendliest kids on the block, but also one of the poorest. His house was very old looking and there were many cracks in the dried paint. He was an only child so he had no brothers or sisters to play with which made him very lonely. His parents were so poor that they could not afford to buy him the things his friends had, like toys or new clothes, and although they were clean, he wore the same clothes almost every day. His fmaily was lucky enough, however, to win a black and white T.V. set which helped to pass the time away, but now he wished he could own the many toys he had seen advertised on it. Jimmy had only a handful of friends, and spent most of his time wishing for the many things he wanted. Whenever he found pretty stones, crystal clear marbles and shiny rings, he would close his eyes tight and begin to wish. He wished on first stars and of course, on falling stars. He wished on almost everything!

One bright sunny morning he heard his mother say as he was awakening, "Hurry up Jimmy, you're late for school again!" Jimmy jumped up hurriedly, dressed and prepared for school. He grabbed his school books and headed out of the door, "Bye!" he said as he dashed off slamming the door behind him. It happened to be trash day and all the garbage cans and trash bags were set out for the trash collectors. As he walked down the street Jimmy came to Thompson's Gift Shop, a store filled to the brim with many strange and unusual articles. In front of the store

was a large yellow-brownish barrel that he couldn't resist
looking into. Inside along with old papers he saw broken chair
and table pieces. These were things he could use for homemade
toys, so he put down his school books and using all of his
strength, he managed to pull out a broken chair leg. At the
same moment a gust of wind picked up some of the papers from the
barrel which went flying off and a very old fashioned oil lamp
covered with dust, fell with a bang to the ground. Jimmy quickly
threw away the broken chair leg for an old object that looked
exactly like 'Aladdin's lamp'!

Jimmy's eyes sparkled and his heart pounded faster and harder
than ever before. It seemed that this was going to be the luckiest
day ever! He hoped that in the lamp there would be a magical
genie living there inside. He used the inside of his shirt tail
to wipe the dust off of the lamp, as he rubbed he closed his eyes
and wished. He rubbed and he scrubbed. Before long the lamp
was wiped clean. He kept rubbing and the old lamp began to shine
so brightly in the sunlight that it hurt his eyes. He waited but
nothing happened. He waited some more, and than began to rub
again, but still nothing happened. He kept rubbing until his
whole arm hurt but it was useless. Jimmy was so upset and angry,
he threw the lamp forcefully to the ground. It bounded a couple
of times and landed in the street where it was smashed beneath
the wheels of a fast moving orange truck. Jimmy's mouth opened
as he just stood there viewing the flat piece of metal on the road
and could feel his eyes begin to water, yet, he wouldn't give in
to his sadness.

Marcus Bruce

He made his way into the wide barrel and once again began
looking inside. He pushed aside the old papers and again found
an unusual item. It was he discovered, a medium sized flawless
crystal ball. He reached carefully into the barrel and pulled
it out. Papers fell out of the barrel and were caught up in
the cool wind and swiftly flew down the street. Jimmy held the
crystal ball up to his eyes and noticed that everything looked
upside down. Suddenly he remembered and said out loud, "Oh
shoot! I'm really going to be late for school!" He placed the
crystal ball inside of his lunch bag, grabbed the school books
and ran quickly off to school.

When Jimmy arrived, he was very, very late. He walked into
the room interrupting class. All of the students turned and
looked at him. "Why are you so tardy Mr. Jumpferjoy?" asked his
teacher in a harsh tone of voice that frightened him. "I, I
woke up late," stammered Jimmy meekly, "then on my way to school
I found a magic lamp in a barrel, but it really wasn't magic at
all." The class found Jimmy's story to be very funny, they began
to laugh and would not stop until the teacher made them. "Stay
out of people's trash cans," she said sharply, "and make sure
you arrive on time from now on, O.K.? "O.K.!" said Jimmy and
held tight to the crystal ball that was inside of his lunch bag.
She asked the class not to embarrass him but poor Jimmy was
already embarrassed. Like a good student Jimmy studied hard in
school, but at the end of the day he felt a tingle of excitement
when the school bell rang. After school he was the first one on
the school bus and the fastest one off. Something unusual was
about to happen and he could feel it.

Once on his block, he ran quickly up the street to his old
weather-beaten looking house. He felt butterflies in his stomach
and happiness in his veins. He went straight to his room, sat
on his bed, and opened the lunch bag. Removing the flawless
crystal ball he stared at it. He loved the way it made everything
look upside down, and noticed upon closer inspection that it was
still a little dusty. He wanted his beautiful crystal ball to
be as clear and as pure as fresh pond water, so, he took the
inside of his dark blue shirt and rubbed until it was smooth and
sparkling clear. He held it close to his eyes and smiled, never
before had he owned such a beautiful object.

Suddenly, the once clear crystal ball began to take on a
greenish tint towards the center. Jimmy was puzzled, he dropped
it on his bed and watched it fill up with bright green smoke.
The misty smoke curled and swirled inside of the crystal ball.
Then it began ot slowly escape from within, and soon filled the
entire room. Jimmy waved his arms and hands to clear the smoke
away, but before he knew what was happening, the smoke vanished
and squatting on his knees before him was a giant genie, strong
and powerful. All alone in his bedroom with a strange greenish
giant. It frightened Jimmy so much that he tried to scream for
help. Although he went through all the motions, no sound came
from his tight throat. Then a horrible thought came to his
mind, "Smashed to death by a seven hundred pound genie." The
monsterous being gave a wide grin showing all of his bright
yellow teeth. His huge head rolled back and he let out a powerful roar of laughter. "Do I frighten you?" he asked in a loud

strong voice. Jimmy stood staring in disbelief. The genie
watched Jimmy with his larger than basketball-size eyes and
spoke again. "This, my friend, is your lucky day!" Jimmy
swallowed to clear his throat and tried to speak but he
couldn't. "What's the matter?" said the genie, "has a cat taken
hold of your tongue?" He reached over and placed his enormous
fingers near Jimmy's small mouth, and produced a fluffy cat
from out of thin air. The genie found it to be very funny and
laughed a loud monster-like laugh. The cat then vanished.
"Are you...," began Jimmy in a dry crackling tone of voice,
"Are you the friendly kind?" "Don't I look friendly?" asked
the huge genie. "Prove it then," said Jimmy gaining his courage
back. "I'll grant thee but three wishes," thundered the genie,
"use them wisely!"

Jimmy could feel the genie's words, at last anything he
wanted could be his! Now for the first time in his whole life
he could have the beautiful and wonderful toys he had seen on
his family's black and white television set. But he stopped
his day dreaming and remembered, there was one wish that would
out wish all other wishes. "Well," he said feeling the beat of
his heart, "I wish for as many wishes as I want!" "Your wish
is granted, Oh, mighty master!" said the genie as he stretched
out his hands and bright sparks of magic flew out of his finger
tips. Jimmy was overjoyed over his first wish and thought to
himself, "Um-m-m, now what should my second wish be?" "I know!"
he said out loud looking at the genie with a sly smile. "I
wish," he closed his eyes tight and said, "I wish, for a real

magic carpet!" The genie stretched forth his hands. "Wait!!"
said Jimmy, "I'm not finished yet." He continued his wish,
"It has to be rainbow colored." "Has master completed his wish?"
asked the genie. "Go ahead," said Jimmy. At once the genie made
a carpet appear flat on the floor in front of Jimmy's bed. "I'd
like to try it out," said Jimmy. "Be my guest," answered the
genie. Jimmy sat in the middle of the carpet and gave it a
command." Rise carpet! The magic carpet quickly rose upward
nearly squishing poor Jimmy into the ceiling. "Down carpet,
down!" he said. The carpet smoothly dropped to the floor.
Jimmy was amused with his new carpet. "For my next wish, I wish
for a telescope," said Jimmy pausing. The genie spread his
hands forward. "Wait!!" said Jimmy. "I want a telescope but
not a regular one. This telescope should be a telescope that
I can use to see anything and everything I want to see at any
time and at any place!" "Is your wish complete, Oh, mighty
master?" asked the genie. "Yeah, that's my wish, I wish for a
telescope of wonder!!!" said Jimmy. The strong and powerful,
magical genie put out his enormous arms and in his large hands
appeared a tiny telescope. The telescope was just the right size
for Jimmy. He loved the look of his new toy. "Wow!" said
Jimmy, "may I try it out?" "If that is what you wish to do Oh,
mighty master," said the smiling genie. "Wow!" said Jimmy putting
the telescope to his eye. "Let me see the world famous Disneyland." At once he was looking at Disneyland with all its different lands and rides. "Let me see my friend Joey," he said and
suddenly he could see Joey riding on his brand new bicycle. Joey

- 7 -

Joey hit a ditch, the bike fell over and Joey landed on the ground.
Jimmy watched Joey walk the bike home and saw him crying on the
way. When Joey entered his house, Jimmy gave him a call on the
phone. "Hi, Joey, are you O.K.?" he asked. "I skinned up my
knees," sobbed Joey. "I know, I saw you," said Jimmy. "Where
were you?" asked Joey still crying. "Oh, I've got to go now,
bye!" said Jimmy and he hung up the phone, and went back into
his room.

"I don't believe it, this is great!" said Jimmy. "I wonder
what else I should wish for?" He thought hard for a moment,
"Well," he said, while thinking aloud, "If I get sick I won't be
able to use my magic carpet or have any fun outside, so, I think
I'll wish for...um," "Medicine?" asked the genie. "I know,"
he said with another one of his joyous smiles. "I wish for one
million magic berries to keep me well whenever I'm sick, and to
keep me from having any pain or injury. To keep me warm when it's
cold and cool when it's hot. Also, I want them to allow me to
breath any atmosphere. These berries must keep me healthy at
all times so I can have many happy days!"

The genie, which towred above him, put out his hands. "Is
this your final wish?" he asked his little master. "There's
nothing else I can think of," said Jimmy. "So be it!" said the
genie. There was a puff of green smoke and greyish berries all
over the place, and the genie, finished with his work, had
disappeared back into the crystal ball. "Oh no!" said Jimmy,
"where am I going to put all of these berries!" Poor Jimmy
couldn't move without stepping on the magic berries. He grabbed

The Amazing Adventures of Jimmy Jumperjoy

a couple of handfuls and stuffed them into his pockets. "I wonder
if I should disturb the genie?" he thought to himself. "No, I
better not, he did enough for one day." Jimmy was upset that he
had forgotten to ask the genie to put the berries into some type
of container. He decided to solve the problem by using large
paper bags from the store to put the berries in. He left his
house in great excitement and ran down the street thinking only
of the new gifts he had received. He wasn't paying any attention
to the stop light and ran straight out into the middle of busy
traffic. There was aloud screeching sound and Jimmy saw a small
green car speeding right at him. The driver slammed on the breaks
but it was too late, the fast moving car hit Jimmy! He flew into
the air and landed hard on the ground. Dazed and hurt, Jimmy
felt terrible while tears streamed down his scratched cheeks.
He saw that a large crowd of people had gathered around him.
Everyone was asking him if he was O.K. Jimmy wanted to speak but
couldn't, the pain was too much for him. Someone in the crowd
said, "Call an ambulance." A tall man in a grey suit pushed his
way throught the crowd. "I'm a doctor," he said, "let me see
if I can help while we're waiting for the ambulance to arrive."
"Let's see," he said as he examined Jimmy. "Fractured ribs, two
broken legs, and possibly internal bleeding." News reporters
seemed to appear out of nowhere. Just then Jimmy remembered
the greyish berries, painfully and slowly he reached into the
nearest pocket and took out one of his magical berries. His movements were very slow and he could hardly breath, but he managed
to put the berry into his sore mouth and chew on it. The sweet

Marcus Bruce

juice of the berry quickly entered his body. The flavor reminded
him of a mixture between blueberries and cherries. Suddenly he
felt fine. "I'm O.K. now!" he said, and stood up. The crowd
was shocked. The doctor was confused and made another examination.
"It felt like your rib cage was broken and it looked like both
your legs were broken," he said. "But now you seem to be alright,
even the scratches on your face have vanished!!!" The news
reporters moaned in disappointment, then left.

An ambulance quickly pulled up and two attendants rushed out.
"Where's the little boy?" asked one of the men. The crowd pointed
to Jimmy who was looking as healthy as could be with a very stupid
grin on his face. "What kind of joke is this?" asked the other
attendant. "It's not a joke," said the doctor. "It's a miracle!!"
"Well," said Jimmy, "it's been nice meeting all of you but I
really must be going home for dinner." Everyone was astonished,
everyone that is, except for Jimmy. He was the only one who
really knew what had happened.

"Jimmy, where have you been?" asked Mr. Jumpferjoy, "we've
been calling you for the last fifteen minutes!" "You didn't go
in my room did you?" asked Jimmy worried. "No, but I was about
to," said Mr. Jumpferjoy. "Your mother thought something might
might have happened to you." "What could happen to me?" asked
Jimmy calmly. "Get ready for dinner," said Mr. Jumpferjoy.
"O.K.," said Jimmy. He washed his hands and enjoyed his dinner
more than ever, being relieved and hungry.

After he ate a delicious meal, Jimmy went straight to his
berry-filled room and rubbed the crystal ball. "I should have

disturbed him the first time," he thought to himself. "Come on out, genie," he said. His room filled up with clouds of green smoke and the large genie appeared. "You called master?" asked the genie. "Could you help me clean up this mess?" asked Jimmy. At once the genie put his hands out and the berries were neatly gathered and placed into large boxes. The genie snapped his fingers and the boxes were stacked in different areas of the room. "That's much better!" said Jimmy. "Have you another wish?" asked the powerful genie. "No, that's all," said Jimmy. With that the genie once more vanished. Jimmy yawned, patted his mouth and looked at the used clock on the wall. "Nine o'clock!" he said to himself. "What a lucky day!" He then put on his pajamas and was soon fast asleep.

Marcus Bruce

Chapter II

THE DREAM

While sleeping comfortably in his small soft bed, Jimmy
Jumpferjoy had the most wonderful dream he ever had and for
the first time this dream was in vivid color. So real it was
as if he wasn't dreaming at all. He found himself walking down
the street in a place full of friendly people, all greeting
him as they passed by. With kind and warm smiles, they shook
his hands and patted him on the back. "Glad to see you here,"
said some. "My aren't you a handsome one," said others. Jimmy
felt like he fit in for once, and that this was his kind of
place. "I've never felt more welcomed!" he said to himself.
"I think I like it here!" As he looked this way and that, his
eyes fell upon a very lovely girl. "Hi there, I like you!"
said the girl. She slowly walked up to Jimmy and held both
of his hands in her's. "What's your name?" she asked pleasantly.
"Jimmy," he answered. "Jimmy what?" she asked very curiously.
"Well, it's Jimmy Jumpferjoy," he answered. "Jumpferjoy?" she
laughed. "What do you do jump for joy all the time?" "No,
I don't," said Jimmy, feeling somewhat put off. "Tell me,
what's your name?" he said. "It's Jilly," she answered. "Do
you have a last name?" asked Jimmy with raised eyebrows. "Why,
yes," she said. "Applejelly." Jimmy couldn't help it, he just
had to laugh. "Jilly Applejelly!" he giggled loudly, "oh boy,
that's funny!"

Then, without knowing why, they both found themselves in
delightful fits of laughter. Jimmy laughed so loud that his

stomach began to ache and tears of laughter rolled down Jilly's
soft cheeks. After the laughter died down, Jimmy gave Jilly
a big hug, and said "Won't you be my friend?" Jilly hugged
Jimmy right back saying, "Of course, silly!" Then she stepped
back and said while wiping her tearful eyes, "Allow me to show
you around, after all you are new here!" "Well, how can I
possibly argue with you?" asked Jimmy. "Good," said Jilly,
"Now look around at the wonders about you. To the left is our
most famous Candy Coat Mountain!" "Sounds delicious," said
Jimmy. "Yes," said Jilly, "as a matter of fact it is. There
is of course a very nice poem about it too!" "Please don't
let me hear it," said Jimmy. "I hate poems, they're too boring!"
"So I'll tell you anyway," said Jilly playfully. "This is how
it goes." Jimmy rolled his eyes upward as Jilly began the poem.
She winked and said, "A special day when all was night, there
came an object twinkling bright. A sparkling rainbow that glowed
in the dark made all the birds of paradise bark. It spread
a wide sparkle over Mystic Hills, past the orange colored ducks
and their fat stouty bills. It hastily sped past the flowing
youth fountain and on the far side of Candy Coat Mountain. It
dug up the ground, nothing was fund but a pot of red peelings
and a sweet smelling sound. Mystical magical dogs flew above
dishing out handfuls of things they called love. That was a
special day when all was night and that sparkling rainbow came
twinkling bright." Jilly took a deep breath. "Well?" she asked.
Jimmy clapped his hands. "It's the very first poem I've ever
really liked." "Come on, Jimmy, there are so many places I'd
like you to see!"

Marcus Bruce

Then a thought came to him. "Wait a minute," he said,
and awoke from his deep sleep. The room was as dark as outer
space without stars. Jimmy turned on the bright lights and
his eyes adjusting, hurt for just a little while, then he took
the crystal ball out from under his bed, and summoned the genie.
"Genie, come out, I want to make a wish," said Jimmy in a dry
tone of voice, while rubbing the crystal ball and sitting on
the edge of his small bed. Instantly the room filled with smoke
and the voice of the genie thundered through the room. "What
would you like, Oh mighty master?" "Sh-h-h," said Jimmy, with
a finger over his lips, "whisper, everyone's asleep!" "What
would you like," asked the genie again only this time in a soft
whisper. "I wish that Jilly Applejelly was real during the
times I want to see her and that I could live in my dream at
night," said Jimmy. "Your wish is granted!" said the genie
in a soft whisper. Jimmy was now able to see the dream directly
in front of him. Jilly stepped out of his dream and into his
room. "Hurry up, Jimmy," said Jilly. "I want to show you the
rest of where I live!"

Up in the night sky, out of Jimmy's window the genie saw
the full moon and something unexpected happened to him. His
face became evil and his whole body looked like hate. "Both
of you," he said in a loud powerful voice. "Sh-h-h!!" said
Jimmy. "Both of you," he continued loudly, "are now under my
command!" Jimmy noticed how the genie had changed and said,
"But I thought you said you were a friendly genie!" The genie
laughed and said, "Oh, I'm friendly most of the time but on

a full moon I'm under a curse to do something wicked or evil."
"What do you mean?" asked Jimmy. "I'm sending you and your
friend to the Sadlands where there is always something terrible
or disgusting happening, and where all the bad things go." He
gave a crazy laugh, scarring poor Jilly to death.

Jimmy ran to the closet and took out his magic carpet and
telescope of wonder. "Well if we have to go, could I at least
take the things you gave me?" asked Jimmy. The genie frowned
and said, "Be you in the Sadlands!" With a flash, sparkle and
clouds of smoke, Jimmy and Jilly found themselves in a land
of terrible odors and dirty skies. The clouds were yellow and
the misty air was brown. Everywhere they could look, the only
thing they saw was pollution.

Jimmy felt nervous to be in a strange filthy looking world.
But somehow his gifts made him feel better. His magic berries
were in his pockets, the magic carpet, rolled up under his arm
and the telescope of wonder in his hand. "Look, Jimmy, over
there!" screamed Jilly. Jimmy looked in the direction that
Jilly was pointing and saw ugly insects four inches long crawling
in their direction. Jilly looked behind and saw the bugs coming
for her and Jimmy. "They're coming after us!" she screamed.
They seemed trapped with nowhere to go. Jimmy grabbed Jilly's
hand, and noticed that she had a bright red ring on her middle
finger. "What kind of ring is that?" "My genie ring, thanks
for reminding me!" she said. "Oh no, you don't!" said Jimmy.
"I have to, they're getting too close!" Jilly said. "Don't
do it!" said Jimmy, "genie's get mean on a full moon!" "Not

Marcus Bruce

mine!" said Jilly and rubbed her red ring. Pink smoke blew
out of nowhere into the dirty brownish air and a very large
woman appeared. "Yes, oh mistress Jilly, how may I help you?"
Jimmy had been surprised to learn that Jilly Applejelly had
a genie but was even more surprised to find the female genie
was kind and gentle. "The bugs are coming after us, if we don't
stop them, they'll walk all over us!" said Jilly nervously.
The great female genie spread forth her long arms and wiggled
her fingers saying to the insects, "You are no longer bugs,
but people!" Suddenly the bugs became people-like but in a
strange way they still resembled bugs. The large crowds of
the bug-people began to grumble in complaint. One of them
stepped up to the genie and said, "Hey, you big dummy, how can
we climb all over people if we are people too?" It shook it's
claw that looked something like a hand and said, "It won't be
any fun!" Some of the bug-people tried climbing over each other
but they just fell down.

Jimmy and Jilly looked at one another and began to laugh.
"This should keep you busy," said the genie. She made a circle
motion with one of her large fingers and there appeared a set
of monkey bars the size of a tall mountain. It didn't take
long for the bug-people to learn what to do with the new creation.
The genie turned to Jilly and asked, "Is everything alright,
now?" "Yes, genie, everything's fine!" Jilly made the O.K.
sign with her fingers and the genie disappeared back into the
ring.

The Amazing Adventures of Jimmy Jumpferjoy

"We must find our way out of this horrible place," said
Jimmy. Jilly watched Jimmy as he rolled open the magic carpet
and said "What if we're not able?" "We're going to get out
of this place if it's the last thing we ever do!" said Jimmy
furiously. "I want you to sit facing the back and keep an eye
on the rear, I'll face the front of the carpet, O.K.?" asked
Jimmy. "O.K!" answered Jilly. "Rise, oh magic carpet," commanded
Jimmy. The carpet swiftly glided upwards and traveled in a
straight path. Jimmy took the telescope of wonder and put it
to his eye. "Show me the way to go!" said Jimmy. He saw a
place where there were thick black clouds.

"I know where to go now, Jilly," said Jimmy, "Just look
for some fluffy black clouds." He tucked the telescope under
his belt and said, "Let's go carpet, move!" With that order
the carpet moved like lightening through the brown sky. As
Jimmy and Jilly looked down, they were glad to be in the air.
For many dangers lurked below. Soon they were flying over Cyclops
Cove and they came across the black clouds Jimmy had seen.
"These are them," said Jimmy, "these clouds are the ones I saw."
"But, Jimmy, I don't see a place to leave!"

Suddenly there was a loud roar, and in front of the carpet
was the huge face of a cyclops monster looking right at them.
Jilly screamed and so did Jimmy. The monster grabbed the carpet
out of mid air with poor Jimmy and Jilly in his awesome grip.
The cyclops carried Jimmy and Jilly into a colossal cave. "Har,
har, har!" laughed the monster blinking the single eye in the
middle of his forehead. "Look what I got!" He held out his

Marcus Bruce

enormous hand and showed his monster family. "Eat 'em now or
eat 'em later?" he asked. "We just ate, stupid!" said his brother
monster with a gargling voice. "We could use a nice desert!"
said the mother monster sitting in the corner of the cave.

Jilly rubbed her ring and whispered, "Hurry genie, hurry,
we need your help!" The monsters started a fire inside of the
cave for what they thought would be a quick snack. The cyclops
that was holding them put them in a huge basket. Suddenly the
pink smoke appeared much to the delight of Jilly and the beautiful genie was ready to help again. "Hey," said the first
monster when the genie appeared, "we have three snacks instead
of two, and this one's bigger too!" "Now we can have seconds!"
said his brother monster. Jilly anxiously told her genie, "these
monsters want to eat us up, you must help us!" Jilly's genie
called out to the mother monster. "You there." "Me?" asked
the mother monster. "No her!" she was pointing her finger at
the mother monster. "What is it that you want?" "Why, a snack
of course," answered the cyclops. "Have you ever eaten cake?"
asked the genie. "What is this cake thing you talk of?" asked
the first monster. The genie put out her arms and wiggled her
fingers. Just outside of the cave entrance appeared a very
large cake that seemed to be never ending. It was as long and
as wide as the Grand Canyon. The greedy monsters pushed and
shoved rushing out of the cave like wild animals. The mother
monster ripped into the cake with her sharp claws and stuffed
it into her open mouth. "It's good!" she roared. The other

monsters joined in. They tore at the cake, and grabbed at it slobbering and gurgling as they too stuffed it into their mouths. Jilly's genie laughed at the sight and said, "Let them eat cake." "They'll be eating that for years," said Jimmy. "I must have that recipe!" said the mother monster inbetween munches. "Can my friends leave now?" asked the genie. "Get lost!" said the first cyclops they had seen.

"Are you O.K. now?" asked the genie. "Thanks to you we are!" said Jilly. The genie then vanished, with a pink puff back into the ring. Jimmy and Jilly sat back to back in the center of the magic carpet. "Rise, oh carpet, and be swift!" said Jimmy. "And make it snappy," giggled Jilly. The carpet quickly left the ground and was off into the brown misty air.

"I'm sure glad they liked the cake!" said Jilly. "I know," said Jimmy, "close call!" He took out his telescope of wonder and said, "which way now?" He saw inside the telescope a grand castle almost completely covered with vines. "O.K., carpet take us to the castle!"

The rainbow colored magic carpet sped past a tall hill covered with dirty dusty papers and used food containers. On another hill not far away, there stood the castle Jimmy had seen. In an old square window there was an odd looking man dressed in a white suit. He stared out of the window being very bored. When he saw the magic carpet approach, he began to laugh uncontrollably. He cracked his knucles and said wildly, "Ah, ha, now to see if my new invention really works!" He dragged his feet across the stone floor as he moved quickly to his

gigantic weather machine. "He, he, he, he, ha!" he laughed
as he flicked switches and pushed over sized buttons. Lights
on the machine flashed and clicking sounds came from within
the very core of the machine.

"Bang, pow, boom!" said the insane scientist, as he laughed
once more and said, "Just watch this!" He pulled a long narrow
lever of the weather machine labeled radiation rain. Huge dark
clouds formed above the magic carpet.

Jimmy looked up at the clouds and said excitedly, "Hey,
where the heck did they come from!?" "I don't know," said Jilly,
"but I don't like the looks of them!" The crazed scientist
looked out of his little square window and was so amused, that
he laughed harder and his unsteady finger couldn't press the
start button on his machine. Jimmy looked into his telescope
of wonder, saw the scientist and what he was up to. "Oh, no!"
he said, "go carpet, go!!" The magic carpet immediately sped
through the unclean air far away from the radiation clouds and
any danger that it could have brought. The evil scientist was
not pleased and stopped his laughter when he saw the carpet
was out of range.

"What the, hey!" he said to himself, "you can't escape
so easily, I won't let you!" He then pushed a button labeled
"follow" on his machine. The large dark clouds began following
the carpet. No matter how fast, how high or how low the magic
carpet went it just couldn't shake the clouds. The gooney
scientist laughed so hard that tiny tears trickled down his
crazed face. He pushed a button labeled "radiation rain drops"

and the dark clouds began to drop their dangerous radiation
rain. The carpet flew wildly from the clouds and it looked
as if nothing could save them. Jilly rubbed her ring and out
poured the pink smoke. The smoke blew off the carpet and Jilly's
poor genie fell quickly towards the ground.

"Oh, no, she's going to die!!" screamed Jimmy. The rain
drops came closer. Jilly frantically rubbed her ring, "come
here, genie, we need you!" The genie appeared between them
on the carpet. "Quick, genie, get rid of those clouds!" The
genie clapped her hands twice and the clouds were gone. "There,
it's safe now!" said the genie.

However, the mad scientist was watching and he saw the
clouds disappear. He pulled a lever labeled "replacement" and
behind them appeared more clouds. "Oh look," said Jilly, "they're
back!" The genie outstretched her arms and they vanished. But
in their place appeared more. "Where are these clouds coming
from?" she asked. Jimmy pointed to the castle. "Over there!"
he said. THe magnificant genie appeared inside the castle
directly behind the wierd scientist. Not knowing that the genie
was in back of him, the scientist was having spasms of laughter.
He laughed so hard that he began to cough and choke. He slapped
his chest while jumping up and down, taking a deep breath he
turned around. What he saw made him cough even harder. He
held his hand over his heart and lost his smile. "Are you quite
finished?" asked the genie. "What the, who the, where did you
come from?" said the mad scientist. The genie did not answer
him, she just snapped her fingers and the machine stopped working.

Marcus Bruce

"What the, hey, you can't do that!"   "I just did!" said the
genie.   "Now I can't have any fun!" said the looney scientist
with an ugly frown on his face.   "You call that fun?" asked
the genie furiously.   "Yes, it's fun. I like to watch people
try to outsmart me," he said with a sinister grin.   "It's great
to see the worried looks on their faces."   He started to laugh,
his dirty teeth chattered, and tiny tears showered down his
droopy cheeks.

Jilly Applejelly's genie was very upset.   "You don't have
to hurt people to have fun!"   The mad scientist hid his in shame.
"Why don't you do something useful, like invent a game or something?"   "I'm afriad, I don't understand," he said.   "Watch
this!" said the genie, and she produced the blueprints for a
simple game.   "You can still outwit people with your games,
you can do this and no one gets hurt!"   "Yes," said the scientist,
"and I shall get to work on a game right now!"   He began to laugh.
"I will call it 'Destiny' and I will have a viewing device to
watch their worried faces."   He laughed and laughed.   "Well,"
said the genie, "that takes care of that," and she was gone
in a pink puff.

Jilly's genie told them about the mad scientist and laughed.
"Now then," she said still giggling, "will I be needed?"   "No
problem now!" said Jilly.   The genie quickly left pink smoke
and all, back into the ring.   Jimmy put the telescope up to
his eye and said, "Show me the way out of here, not the way
to danger!"   There came into view, a land full of snow and ice.
"O.K., carpet," said Jimmy, "snow covered land here we come!"

As they drifted closer and closer to the snow region, Jilly
began to complain. "We didn't bring any warm clothes, or did
you forget?" "I'm feeling pretty cold too," said Jimmy. "Got
any bright ideas before we freeze to death," said Jilly. "The
berries!!!" screamed Jimmy. "What berries?" asked Jilly. "Why
did it take so long for me to remember the berries!" said Jimmy.
"Are you going to tell me about the berries or not?" said Jilly.
Jimmy took two magical berries out of his pocket. "One for
you and one for me!" He handed her a berry. "Now just take
a bite and taste the flavor of blueberries and cherries dance
across your taste buds." Jilly ate her berry. "Hey, this is
good!" she said, "but how's it going to keep us warm?" "These
are magic berries, that's how!" said Jimmy.

As they approached the icy area the berries warmed their
bodies. The sky was a bluish-grey and the wind whipped round
about the carpet. It all looked very cold and chilly but it
didn't bother Jimmy or Jilly. They held tight to the outer
edge and went for a wild ride on a rippling carpet. Great snow
clouds came into sight and out of them came large white snowflakes.

Jimmy was enjoying the feel of the snow tickling his skin
and Jilly was having the time of her life. They were having
so much fun that they didn't realize the carpet was sinking
lower and lower from the heavy weight of the snow. "This is
fantastic, Jimmy!" said Jilly. "What?" he asked, "I can't hear
you!" The vicious wind howled so loud that they could hardly
hear each other. The snow was so thick that they could hardly
see. Jilly realized that they were sinking and said, "Jimmy,

Marcus Bruce

we're going down!" "What?" he said, "I can't hear you." She
answered, "We're going down, I think we're going to crash!"
"What trash?" asked Jimmy. "I can't hear you!!" said Jilly
and before they knew it they were sitting on snow covered ground.
They were in the middle of a blizzard nearly pushed over by
the powerful wind. "My carpet is buried under all this snow!"
said Jimmy anxiously. "Well, dig it out!" said Jilly. There
was a loud roar, but it seemed as if the wind was making all
of the noise.

What Jimmy and Jilly didn't know was that they were being
surrounded by the frosted ice people. One of the creatures
let out an ear piercing scream. The others joined in making
Jilly so nervous she grabbed hold of Jimmy. "You have come
here!" roared the leading ice man. "But why?" Jimmy looked
nervously at Jilly and said, "Oh boy, here we go again!" "Why
do you come here?" asked another roaring ice man. "It was an
accident!" yelled Jimmy, "my carpet got an overload of snow
and we fell to the ground." "You are not telling the truth!"
roared the leading ice man. "But I am!" said Jimmy, "just ask
Jilly!" "You're nothing but a pair of nosey humans!" yelled
an ice woman. "Let's get rid of them!" said a smaller ice man.
"Jilly," said Jimmy, "I think it's time for you to call out
your genie!"

She rubbed her ring, and instantly the genie came out of
the pink smoke to help her friends out of trouble once more.
"Another problem?" she asked. "The ice people are cold blooded,
they think we're here to cause trouble!" said Jilly. "But

we're not," said Jimmy, "we crashed!" "Let's get those humans!"
said the leader. "They did you no harm!" said the genie. "No,"
said the leader, "but if we let them stay they will. All the
humans do is cause harm!" "These two are just trying to find
their way home!" said the genie angrily. "Are you telling the
truth?" asked the ice woman. "I am," said the genie. "She's
a liar!" said the leader, "tie them up!!" The other ice people
gathered ice rope and came at Jilly, Jimmy and the genie while
the leader sharpened his ice spear. "I have a surprise for
you!" said the genie. She snapped her large fingers and the
ice rope turned into different colored ice stuff. Caught by
surprise, the ice people wondered what had happened. "What
is this sick looking icy stuff?" asked a small ice man. "It
may look bad to you ice men, but wait until you taste it," said
the genie. The ice woman was the first to try it out. "I like
to eat this strange ice," she said, "it is good to me!" Soon
every ice man was smiling and glad to have such a good experience.

"It's a good thing they liked Popsicles," said Jilly. "I
thought they would," said the genie. "Is everything set now?"
"Well, everything but the snow on the carpet," said Jimmy. The
genie made a circle with her finger, the ice and snow disappeared
from the carpet. "Thank you, muchly," siad Jimmy. "Don't men-
tion it!" answered Jilly's genie, and vanished. "Ready, Jilly?"
asked Jimmy. "Ready!" she said. "Float magic carpet, float!"
said Jimmy and the carpet started to float very slowly upward.
"Goodbye!" said Jilly to the ice people. The entire group of

Marcus Bruce

ice men wildly yelled and roared. Jimmy smiled and waved to
them, then he took out his telescope of wonder. "Please, please,
please show us the way out of this weird place, please!" In
his telescope he saw nothing but darkness. "There's something
wrong with this thing!" he said, "it's not working!" We probably
have to go to some kind of dark place in order to leave here,"
said Jilly. "I hope you're right!" said Jimmy, "you heard it
carpet, find the darkest place in the land!" The magic carpet
was off and speeding swiftly to an unknown dark area.

Before they knew it, they began to approach the darkest
place Jimmy had ever seen in his life. The air grew thicker
and the light grew dimmer. The closer they got the darker it
got, almost like passing through a dark, black fog. "I think
we're lost," muttered Jimmy. "No, we're not!" said Jilly, "Look!"
From out of the darkness came a light moving toward the carpet
at a fantastic rate of speed. It charged forward and seemed
to be cutting right through the dark fog. The intense light
was so bright and blinding that Jimmy squenched his eyes. Then
it crashed right into the carpet. Glittering sparkles of light
specks shot in every direction, and in one instant Jimmy was
safe. Back at his house in his room, he and Jilly were seated
upon his magic carpet.

Jimmy stood up and jumped in the air, "We're home!" he
yelled. "We're back!" Jilly gave him a big hug. His room
was just as he left it, dark rather small, and a few scattered
clothes here and there. Jimmy said goodbye to Jilly then lay
back in his bed and Jilly went into the dream. When he fell

The Amazing Adventures of Jimmy Jumpferjoy

asleep, he met Jilly and she introduced him to some of the people
there. They talked about what had happened in the sadlands
and about how they thought they were trapped for good. In the
morning on a Saturday, Jimmy washed up and was the first one
at the table for breakfast. But he didn't realize he had been
gone so long and his parents were very angry. "Where have you
been?" demanded his mother. "Out with Joey?" he asked. "Don't
you lie to me!" she said. "I called Joey's mother and she told
me she hadn't seen you!" "Oh," said Jimmy embarrassed. "If
you think I'm angry, wait 'til you see your father." Jimmy
knew his father had a bad temper and was hoping that he wouldn't
return home until very late. He ate his breakfast and went
to the park. While he was at the park, he began to see all
that the genie had done to him. "I always wanted a genie but
this one is too much trouble," he thought to himself. "Maybe
I should get rid of that stupid crystal ball! Who wants a genie
that sends you away to the sadlands? When my father gets home
it's all over! How am I going to explain it, he'll never believe
me! What the heck do I do now? Is it O.K. to use my genie
or will he just send me back to the sadlands? Well," he said
to himself while heading back home, "I'd rather be in the sadlands than face my father!"

In his room Jimmy took out the crystal ball. He looked
at it for a while then boldly started to rub it. "I don't care
what you do to me now," he said, "I lose either way." "Just
show your stupid face!" The room filled with green smoke and
the genie appeared. "I'm sorry, Master Jimmy, I didn't tell

Marcus Bruce

you about the full moon until too late. I've sent many of my
masters to the sadlands but most have never returned. The last
master somehow escaped with the help of a witch, how did you
leave?"

Jimmy just looked at the genie. "I don't feel like talking
about it. You're O.K. now, aren't you?" he asked. "Yes,"
thundered the genie. "Good," said Jimmy, "because I was about
to throw you away!"

Jimmy's father came home in a very bad mood and when he
found out Jimmy was home he went straight to Jimmy's room.
"Jimmy!" yelled Mr. Jumpferjoy. "Where have you been?" Jimmy
tried to lie, but it didn't work. Mr. Jumpferjoy was angry
and wanted to hear the truth. Mr. Jumpferjoy ended up telling
Jimmy he was not allowed out for the number of days he was
missing, and that the only thing he could have for dinner was
cabbage. And Jimmy didn't like the taste of cabbage.

When Jimmy went back to his room he looked sad. "Maybe
we shouldn't be so hard on him," said Jimmy's mother. "If we
don't, he might try to run away again!" said Mr. Jumpferjoy.

Jimmy sat on his lone bed and took out his crystal ball.
"O.K.," he said, "now that that's all over I guess I should
call out my genie." The genie came out of the gree clouds of
smoke and Jimmy spoke. "I'd like to have a very large pizza
for dinner tonight and for desert I'd like to have a strawberry
shortcake, but, um, pizza first!" The genie held out his hands
and a table appeared in front of Jimmy with a tasty cheese pizza.

He loved his dinner and enjoyed his desert. After his meal
Jimmy had the genie clear away the mess.

    "This is the life!" said Jimmy. He gave a big yawn and
fell asleep on his bed. "Hey, there you are!" said a familiar
voice, "I've been waiting for you!" It was Jilly Applejelly.
"I've got to show you around, there's so many places you've
got to see!"

Chapter 3 -   JILLY APPLEJELLY'S WONDERFUL WORLD

"There are a lot of places that I'd like to show you, but first we must stop at my house!"

said Jilly anxiously. Jimmy dragged his feet, he wasn't in any hurry. But for Jilly he

was moving much too slow. "Come on Jimmy!" she said. "I've got to show you my

matter conversion machine!" "What's a conversion machine?" he asked. "I'll show

you!" she said and with that she broke in a run. Together they ran and walked close to

three miles before Jilly announced, "Well, here we are! This is my house!" "Are your

parents home?" asked Jimmy. "No," said Jilly, "they live in their own house, silly!"

"That's yours?" he asked, "That big thing is your home?" Jimmy stared wide eyed with

disbelief at a huge, colorful Victorian house. Fancy designs decorated her home.

In the front yard she had a large rose garden full of many different kinds of roses.

Surrounding her big house was a tall iron gate, and in front of the gate were two large

marble lion statues. The clean windows on Jilly's house were framed with stained glass.

The walkway to the house was in mosaic tile and the wide front porch was of the finest

crystal. A small stream trickled through her front yard. Over the stream was a sky blue

bridge decorated with white wooden flowers. The shingles on her rooftop were solar

cells which supplied all her heat and electrical energy needs.

"No way, I just can't believe that all this is yours!" said Jimmy. "Let's go inside,"

said Jilly. "I'm not going in there!" said Jimmy. "I don't even believe that this is your

house!" "What do you mean?" asked Jilly frustrated, "Don't you believe me?" "No!"

said Jimmy. "But I'm your friend, you have to believe me!" she said. Jilly grabbed

Jimmy's left hand and spoke firmly, "Listen Jimmy, this is not your world. This is not

your land!" she looked deep into his eyes as she spoke, "Things are different here.

I bet you don't even have flying unicorns in your land!" said Jilly. "Flying unicorns?"

said Jimmy. "Come here!" said Jilly and she led Jimmy around her house to a grand

back yard. Eating the green leaves on the tall bushes were three young unicorns

with large wings. One was light blue, one pink and the other was a smokey black.

"Unbelievable!" said Jimmy, "I must be dreaming!" "You are!" said Jilly. "Now do

you believe this is my home?" "Well," said Jimmy scratching his head in confusion,

"what can I say?"

"Wait 'till you see my matter conversion machine!" said Jilly, "You won't believe that

either!" They went back around to the front and Jilly touched a purple button on the

gate. The marble lions turned and looked directly at Jimmy with large glassy eyes. A

chill went through his body. "It's ok!" said Jilly, cheerfully, "he's with me!" Jimmy

gulped, cleared his throat and looked about nervously. The stone lions turned, faced

front and became motionless as before.

As Jimmy walked up the pathway toward Jilly's huge home he couldn't help thinking

about his small unkempt house with flakes and cracks in the paint, a front screen door

with half the screen falling out, the broken window in his kitchen and his front yard

covered with weeds. Even though he was made to clean up, there was almost always

some type of litter in the yard.   Surrounding his little house was a wooden fence with most of the wood missing. There were no marble lions to protect his home from anyone who would want to rob him. Jimmy wondered to himself, "How would I feel if I could have my very own house, a large house filled with trap doors and secret sliding panels!" He smiled pleasantly at this thought.

"Hey," he thought to himself, "I could have a home all to myself. I could have a house, a boat, a car or anything! Why didn't I realize it? I've got a genie at hand! I could have a house if I wanted to!" "But," he thought to himself, "how could I hide it from my parents and friends. My mother and father would be curious and want to know where it came from. They would want to know where I got the money to buy it. They might think I'm a thief, and probably would think the money was stolen. They'd hate me! I don't think I could live all alone in a big house anyway, and I know I couldn't bring my parents to live there!" "Oh, well" he thought with a sigh, "when I get older I'll buy a house with trap doors!"

Inside Jilly's big house it was like being in a museum. Everything was very fancy. Most of her things were made of pure gold and silver. "Wow!" said Jimmy, "this is the biggest house I've ever seen in my whole life!" "Do you really like it?" asked Jilly in a snobby type of voice." "Follow me dear and I shall show you something that will absolutely astound you!" They walked down the long narrow hallway in Jilly's mag-nificant house and at the end of the hallway they came to a steep stairway. The stairs led to the next level down and into a smaller room. In the room there was a very small machine.

"There it is! said Jilly Applejelly. "That's it!" said Jimmy unimpressed. "So what?" he said, "What's the big deal?" "Don't you like it?" asked Jilly, "It's my favorite toy!" "What do you do with it?" he asked. "Watch!" said Jilly. She picked up a magazine called "You're The Boss". She grabbed a pair of scissors and cut out a picture of a doll house. "Isn't this a pretty doll house?" asked Jilly. Jimmy rolled his eyes. "Is that a copy machine?" he asked. "No," said Jilly. "Then what is it?" he asked. "It's my very special matter conversion machine" she said, "Take a look at it."

Jilly placed the paper cutout into a slot and flicked a switch. Lights blinked, strange music sounded, the smell of lemonade came out of it and a small beam of light projected into midair. The beam of light drew a small outline of the doll house which became larger and larger 'till it was about three feet tall and two feet wide. It was large enough for several large dolls. The light, which was a brilliant blue, began to take on the colors that were in the magazine. Particles of light began to settle and then, right there on the floor before Jimmy, was a beautiful solid wooden doll house. The machine lights went off, the music stopped and the lemonade smell vanished.

"Wow!" said Jimmy "Can I try that!" "No!" said Jilly. "Why not?" he asked. "Because!" she said. "Because why?" asked Jimmy. "You didn't say you liked my doll house!" said Jilly, "which means you've been very rude!" "I'm sorry!" said Jimmy, "I didn't mean to be rude." "Oh, don't get so excited!" said Jilly "I'm only teasing you!"

She started to giggle and ran quickly out of the room. "Hey Jilly, where're you going?" said poor confused Jimmy. He ran out after her but to his astonishment she had disappeared. "Hey Jilly!" he yelled loudly. "Jilly!" screamed Jimmy. The sound of his voice echoed throughout the halls. "Jilly Apple...help!" screeched Jimmy as he felt something grab hold of his shoulder. "Help!!" screeched Jimmy frantically. "You big chicken!" said a young voice. "Jilly Applejelly!" said Jimmy, "you scared me!" "Oh yeah?" said Jilly "Now I'm going to tickle you!" "You wouldn't," he said backing away. "Watch me!" she said. She wiggled her little fingers under Jimmy's arms and he started to laugh like he had never laughed before. He laughed so hard that the echoes were bouncing off of each other. He laughed so hard that big salty tearsdrops slid down the sides of his round cheeks. He laughed so hard that his stomach began to hurt and then he laughed some more.

"Now, dear boy," said Jilly in her very snobby voice, "you may use my utterly fantastic machine, under one condition. "What do you mean?" asked Jimmy wiping the laughter tears from his eyes. "You must not break the dear thing, understand?" "Ok, I won't break it!" said Jimmy smiling. "You must swear that you will not break it, now or ever" said Jilly sharply. "I swear that I will not break it now or ever," repeated Jimmy. "It is not polite to swear!" said Jilly. "You have been quite rude to me once more, dear boy!" "What?" said Jimmy, "you're crazy!" "I, dear boy am only teasing you, have I made myself perfectly clear?" she said, "Do you know what the word 'joke' means?" "Yeah!" said Jimmy. "Well, I have merely been joking Jimmy!" she said and picked up her magazine.

"Now you may pick and chose the thing that you like the very best." said Jilly. Jimmy
took hold of the thick magazine and thumbed through it. "Let's see," said Jimmy, "here
are some great army toys, and there's a movie camera, a projector and a movie screen,
or, I could have a superhero costume, or a laser pistol, or a package of fruit punch gum."
He quickly turned the page. "Here's something for you, Jilly, a powder pink Easter
bunny with violet eyes!" "I already have one," said she. "Well," said Jimmy, "there is
a lot to choose from!" "Here's a swimming pool submarine, and pet robot, and night
specs for seeing in the dark, and a freeze gun to scare my enemies."

"Will you hurry up and chose something!" said Jilly anxiously, "you're taking all day!"
"I can't make up my mind!" said Jimmy, "Can I have them all?" "Do you want to break
my machine? asked Jilly. "Couldn't I pick at least two?" asked Jimmy hopefully. "One
at a time," said Jilly. "Ok," said Jimmy happily. "First I'll pick the superhero
costume." Jilly Applejelly handed Jimmy the sissors and Jimmy carefully cut out the
costume.

"What if it won't fit?" he asked. "One size fits all!" said Jilly, "It's shrinkable and
stretchable." "Oh!" said Jimmy and went back to cutting out the design. "Now place
the cutout into this slot," said Jilly seriously, "and flick this switch over here." Jimmy
did as he was instructed to do and the machine's lights flickered and flashed and a
rainbow of colors appeared. The smell of cherry juice filled the air and a beautiful sound
of music came with it. Suddenly a brilliant fiery red beam created the outline of the
costume. The image grew larger and larger until it was just about the size of Jimmy.

Small particles of light settled into place and the colors of the costume were drawn with light. The material became solid and fell gently to the ground.

Jimmy quickly picked it up and put it over his arm. "Where's your guest room?" he asked "I don't have one," said Jilly. "All these rooms in your house and you don't have a guest room?" he asked. "Why do you want a guest room, anyway," she asked curiously. "I want to change into my superhero costume," he said. "you don't need a guest room for that," said Jilly, "it's stretchable, remember?" "Oh," said Jimmy, "I get it" He was able to put the costume right over his play clothes, and, it fit perfectly.

"Hey, look at me!" he said, "I'm super Jimmy!" "Faster than a speeding bullet, more powerful than a train that can't be stopped. Look up in the air, it's a bird, it's a plane, say hey, it's Jimmy Jay! The friendliest, the coolest, the smoothest, the smartest and the cutest crime fighter of all times. And never chicken, not even afraid of Jilly Applejelly. Even when she acts crazy!" "Oh yeah?" said Jilly, "look who's acting crazy now!" "Does it really work Jilly?" he asked. "Let's see!" she said and quickly picked up a small rubber ball. She threw the ball right at Jimmy but surprisingly the costume was surrounded by a force field so the ball never even came close to hitting Jimmy.

"I like it, I like it!" said Jimmy nodding his head. "Try flying!" said Jilly. Jimmy bent his knees and the next thing he knew he was floating slowly around the room! He waved to Jilly and she waved back to him. "Hey Jilly!" he said from above. "Can I jump over your house now?" "No!" said Jilly, "you might frighten my unicorns!"

"Ok," said Jimmy and came down to join Jilly on the floor. "Wowee!" he said grinning. "I really do feel super!" Do you have any crime around here?" Jimmy asked Jilly. "There's no such thing as crime here. Not one person here believes that there is crime anywhere. In this land no one ever gets sick, no one gets killed and no one dies."

"Never?" asked Jimmy. "Never!" said Jilly. "As a matter of fact, no one ever really gets old here either." "How come?" asked Jimmy. "The youth fountain, remember the poem I told you!" "Then how will I ever really use my super hero costume?" "You can use it to play in," said Jilly, satisfied with her answer. "To play in?" asked Jimmy sadly, "I want to be a real crime fighter!" "You're out of luck kid!" she said "no crime, no crime fighter!" "Well, can I at least get the second thing I wanted?" he asked hopefully. "Just one more and that's all!" she said.

"I'll go for the freeze gun, it'll go with my super hero costume!" said Jimmy. I'll make criminals stop in their tracks and capture them in the act." "Ok," she said, "but hurry up, I want to show you around!" Jimmy Jumpferjoy cut out the little freeze gun and placed it into the slot. The machine started up. The lights sparkled and flashed a yellowish color and the smell of fresh cut oranges now floated in the air. The golden tones of music danced high and low while a bright florescent green beam of light began to draw the outline of the gun.

- 41 -

When it was all over, he had a weapon that could do no physical harm to anyone. It was a teardrop shaped object, silverish in color and fit right in the palm of Jimmy's hand. There were no buttons and there was no trigger, nothing on it that he could see that would make it work. "How do you do this?" he asked Jilly. "Just point it at something moving and it will freeze it." she said, "Watch!" She picked up the rubber ball and threw it up into the air. "Now!" she said. He pointed the freeze gun at the ball and it stayed in the air. "How far will this thing shoot?" he asked. "As far as you want!" she answered. "Put it in the utility belt on your costume!" "Why?" asked Jimmy. "I want to show you around!" she said excitedly and leave your costume on!"

"Where are we going to go?" he asked, while putting away his freeze gun. "Candy Coat Mountain range!" said Jilly, "I'll take one of my flying unicorns and you can use your super powers!" "I'll fly there?" he asked. "Right," she said, "By the way, anything in your utility belt will shrink with the suit." Before long they were on their way. Jilly Applejelly took the smokey black unicorn and being very young, it was very strong and flew with ease above the houses and trees. Right behind Jilly flew Jimmy, his arms were straight in front of him and his legs held straight and stiff. His glittering blue cape flapped in the cool wind and from his utility belt he was able to find special windproof black rimmed water repellent glasses.

Below him he could see the city which was not at all like his own. The buildings here were round and looked like sponge rubber. There were many odd looking trees. Some looked as if they had money where the leaves were supposed to be. Others looked as though they had many different colored lights. Some of the flying creatures also looked pretty strange. Just in front of him were several fishes with gills, scales and long thin wings which fluttered like bee wings. He also saw some flying dogs just as in the poem Jilly had told to him. "Did you see those weird creatures, Jilly?" he asked. "What weird creatures?" she asked in confusion. "Flying fishes and dogs!" he said. "What's so unusual about that" she answered, "I see them all the time!"

The clear sky was a beautiful sea green, the air smelled like cotton candy and large clouds were pink and fluffy like spun sugar. This whole land was wonderful, strange and new to Jimmy. Some of the things were the same as in his world, however, there were other things that were very odd to him. He wondered if perhaps there was another part of this land he hadn't seen yet that was not as beautiful and not so enchanting. Maybe, just maybe it would have horrible monsters, like the ones in the sadlands. Perhaps somewhere hiding in the shadows were ugly goblins or evil witches ready to strike.

If there were creepy evil things lurking about little Jimmy was ready for them. He had his super costume and his automatic freeze gun, no one would be able to frighten him. Nothing would even touch him either, not with the force field surrounding the costume. The flying unicorn flapped it's wings harder, flew swifter and took the lead way far ahead of Jimmy. Jilly turned around and laughed, "I'm winning!" "Not for long," he said powerfully. He pulled his arms back and flew much further than the unicorn.

Jilly, not one to be out done, patted the flying unicorn and it sped out in front of Jimmy once more. She pulled the reigns back and gently kicked its sides. "Come on Smokey let's go!" she yelled, "yippee!!" The young unicorn zoomed like a bird flying up and down, side to side. It made great swoops and did so many loops that Jilly became dizzy and suddenly lost her grip. Her body was hurled forward. She flipped in midair and was headed non-stop toward the sharp rocks on the ground below. Jilly became frightened. She let out a screech that would scare even the ice people. Sweat formed on her forehead and her brain was fogged. She screamed again and passed out.

Jimmy noticed just how quickly she was falling and he immediately took action. He reached into his utility belt and pulled out his freeze gun, aimed it at Jilly and fired. Her limp body was quickly frozen in time and space. Everything else was fine. The fishes were flying and so were the dogs, the river was flowing and the wind was blowing. Absolutely everything was as usual except for a frozen Jilly Applejelly suspended in mid-air. The pet unicorn was slowly flying away from her and about to make a great escape when Jimmy turned and fired at it also.

The winged beast, like Jilly, was motionless like a statue stopped in the air. All time was frozen for the dark animal. Jimmy quickly flew to Jilly and floated her safely to the ground. The he grabbed the unicorn and did the same. "Oh, no!" thought Jimmy, somewhat worried. I don't even know how to unfreeze them!" He examined his freeze gun and could find no trace of an opening. "Wow, what will I do?" he thought as he looked around, "where can I get help?" He flew his highest into the sky only to see

wilderness in every direction.   There was nothing he could do, even as a super hero.
He was powerless.

Again he looked over his weapon and as his sad eyes slowly scanned the front, back and
sides he saw it was as solid as steel and as smooth as glass.   Just then a thought entered
his mind.   "What if I point the back of it at them.   Wouldn't that reverse the freezing
process?"   He took the freeze gun and pointed the blunt back end at the winged unicorn
and then at Jilly.   Sure enough they began to unfreeze.   Slowly at first, as if in slow
motion.   Jilly moved her arms up and down while the winged unicorn moved its neck
and wings also in slow motion.

"What happened?" asked Jilly, "The last thing I remember I was falling."   "And you
would have died if I hadn't saved you!" he said clenching his fist.   "Jimmy!" said Jilly
sternly, "I told you before that people don't die here!"   "But you were falling!" he said
excitedly, "and you would have hit the ground!"   "I would have bounced!" she said,
"the ground is flexible." "Even those sharp rocks?" said Jimmy wondering what was
going on.   "Yes, even the sharp rocks," said Jilly.

She climbed back on top of the flying unicorn and flew on over toward the nearest cliff.
"Stay there!" said Jilly, "watch this!"   She rolled a large boulder over the side of the cliff
and it dropped with all of it's massive weight quickly toward the ground.   When it hit the
ground instead of breaking into millions of pieces as expected, it bounced, almost all the

way up to Jilly. The whole ground rippled like water leaving Jimmy with his mouth wide open! When Jilly came back to Jimmy she said "See, I told you!" "Well, why did you scream, why did you panic like that?" "It tickled my stomach and made me feel nervous. That's why I was yelling like that!" said Jilly.

"Well, if you were in my world, I would have saved you!" said Jimmy anxiously. "If I was in your world" she said, "I wouldn't have fallen off of a flying unicorn!" "Can't argue with that," said Jimmy, "How much further to Candy Coat Mountain?" "We are here!" said Jilly, "this is it! What is it they say, um….. keep looking, for the things you seek may be directly in front of you!" "Well," said Jimmy with a sigh of relief, "now where do we go?" "Follow me!" said Jilly smiling.

Onward they went, traveling past little lakes and barren meadows, riding the air currents swiftly and easily. Never looking back, never stopping. A gallant smokey black unicorn leading the way and a curious super hero courageously following. Below Jimmy could see small farms and animals he never dreamed could exist. "Where are you taking us?" he asked, not knowing when this journey would ever end. "We're going to Candy Coat National Park!" she said, "It's lots of fun!" "What's there?" he asked. "It's a surprise!" said Jilly. They flew over flowered meadows and woods. When the long journey had ended, Jimmy found himself in a beautiful green country side. He saw large redwood trees with butterflies the size of busses.

A sparkling clear river flowed gently over a bed of clear rocks. "Try one," said Jilly. "Try what?" he asked. "One of the pebbles!" she said. "This place is loaded with crystals!" said Jimmy. "Those are not crystals!" laughed Jilly, "silly, that's rock candy, try one." He bent over and picked up a fairly large chunk and took a great big crunchy bite. It wasn't exactly what he had expected because the rock candy wasn't that hard. But it was the most delicious piece of candy he had ever tasted. "Not far from here is a ginger- bread house, and the girl that lives there doesn't mind if people eat her house!" said Jilly. "Oh, I'm afraid I shouldn't eat too much candy" said Jimmy apologetically, "it's bad for my teeth!" "Not here!" said Jilly, "nothing is bad for you here! This is not your land! You keep forgetting that!" "You're absolutely right!" he said, "I'm sorry, I made a mistake!"

"Now before I take you to the uncharted forest, I must warn you, it's very easy to get lost there so stay close!" She grabbed the reigns of the unicorn and showed the way. The towering redwood trees in the uncharted forest were almost side by side. The area was dark, damp and had a very sweet scent. Large molasses swamps seemed to be every- where.

Jilly led Jimmy down a very slim and narrow passageway on foot, which was the only road and only way to travel at this point. "I don't know about you Jilly," said Jimmy, "but this place looks pretty creepy to me. "Nonsense," she said bravely, "this is the safest place in the whole area! Beside, what are you worried about, you're a superhero!" "I know," said Jimmy nervously "but it still looks pretty creepy."

Further and further into the deep, dark, damp woods traveled a lone boy and girl. They

traveled on foot through the molasses swamps. Their feet sank slowly as if in liquid

quicksand, or sticky mud. It made walking very difficult. "How much further?" asked

Jimmy when his legs became tired. "Not too much further!" said Jilly pulling her foot

out of a sticky mess. "Look!" she said pointing. Jimmy saw a small house, yellowish

brown in color with white frosting for a rooftop. The house looked mouth watering and

delicious!" "Is it real?" asked Jimmy. "It most certainly is!" said Jilly excitedly, "and

there's my friend, Fluidica Dewdrop!"

Sure enough, out of the gingerbread house came a little girl about the same height as Jilly

Applejelly. Her face was somewhat thin and her complexion was bluish. Her smooth

ears were pointed at the tips and the eyes set in her head were like that of a deer, very

large and brown. She reminded Jimmy of the pictures he had seen of elves in his story

books. He became a little frightened at the thought of meeting a living elf.

"This is my new friend Jimmy Jumpferjoy, I'm showing him around." said Jilly. "Hello

Jimmy," said Fluidica in a high squeaky voice, "want a bite of my house?" "No thank

you Fluidica," he answered. He scratched his head and then said, "How are you?" "I'm

enjoying life and nature, how are you?" she asked. "Just fine!" said Jimmy. "I'm going

to take him exploring and I wondered if you had any new ideas where I could take him,"

said Jilly.

"How about Valley One?" asked Fluidica. "Boring!" answered Jilly. "I know!" said
Fluidica quickly in her squeaky voice, "I discovered a cave only four miles down stream
of Sugar Water River!" "Really?" said Jilly, "then show us the way!" "But we'll have
to fly there," said Fluidica anxiously. "It's Ok!" said Jilly, "smokey's not tired, are you
smokey?" The unicorn shook its head from side to side. "Follow me then!" said
Fluidica as she leaped up. Magical dust trailed behind her. "She is a fairy!" whispered
Jimmy under his breath.

After flying a great distance they were able to land. The cave entrance was the biggest,
the largest, the absolutely most enormous opening Jimmy had ever seen. Small birds
were flying quickly in and out of it, for they made it their home. "I hope whatever else
lives there is smaller than the cave!" said Jimmy. "Let's find out!" screamed Fluidica
and with ease she swiftly flew inside. Jilly was in next with her flying unicorn, smokey
and Jimmy, although still quite nervous, went in after them. It was dark inside like being
in the mouth of a whale at midnight. Only the sparkles from Fluidica's magic dust were
able to light the way. The cave was large enough to hold several large rockets. It
made Jimmy feel like at any moment something vicious would jump out and eat them all.
Soon the cave began to smell like sour milk. The air was getting stuffy and Jimmy
began to have second thoughts about whether or not this was a wise journey. After all,
neither Jilly nor Fluidica had ever been here before.

"Hey, you guys!" said Jimmy, "where do you think we're going?" "To the edge of eternity!" screamed Fluidica and the high pitched voice seemed to echo endlessly. "We're calling it an endless pit!" laughed Jilly, "forward instead of downward!" "No, we're falling backwards instead of forward," yelled Fluidica and giggled like a chipmunk. "What do you say Jimmy?" asked Jilly curiously. "I want to go home!" came the frightened voice of Jimmy. "Jimmy, you must be the biggest chicken I know!" laughed Jilly. "Hey, I didn't say that!" said Jimmy surprised. "You did too!" said Jilly, "I heard you. Didn't Jimmy say he wanted to go home Fluidica?" "That's right, I heard him!" answered Fluidica.

"It sounded like me but it wasn't me!" said Jimmy, "I'm not kidding!" "Jimmy's an ugly little boy who picks his nose!" said a voice that sounded like Fluidica's. "That wasn't a very nice thing to say, Fluidica!" said Jilly angrily, "Jimmy's my friend!" "Why, Jilly Applejelly!" exclaimed Fluidica, "you know me better than that. I would never say something that rude!" "You smell like a rotten egg and so does Jimmy!" said a voice that sounded exactly like Jilly's. "Somebody's playing tricks on us!" said Jimmy, "Nobody talk until we leave this part of the cave!"

But even as they remained silent the voices continued to echo insults at the trio. The air became silent and the sound of a strong wind whistled up ahead. Fluidica looked nervously behind her to see if the friends were still close by. Howling winds echoed louder and louder as Jimmy, Jilly and Fluidica slowly drifted to an unknown cave area.

Strange laughter suddenly came out of nowhere and almost seemed to know…… It was giving an ice cold chill to the three. "Let's go back!" said Jimmy, "right now!" "I'd be glad to!" said Jilly, "Are you going too, Fluidica?" "We can't turn back!" she said frantically. "Why not?" said Jimmy. "The air!" answered Fluidica, "It's like a vacuum!" "We're being sucked into a tunnel!" said Jilly, with a very worried expression on her face. The powerful wind pulled and tugged them quickly forward, spinning and whirling them around. The winged beast let out a wild and frantic sound, for it too **began to panic.**

"There is no escape" echoed a ghostly voice, "You are all doomed!" Then its deep laughter changed into a cackle like that of an evil witch. "Hey Jimmy!" screamed Jilly, "remember I called you a chicken?" "How could I forget!" yelled Jimmy. "Well I take it back!" she said with large tears slowly forming in her eyes. Faster and faster they went, spinning, twisting moving forever forward. Onward endlessly, not knowing where this whirl wind was taking them. Head over heals they tumbled losing more and more control of their little bodies.

They were whipped by the wind, flipping and flopping, swirling round and round until they finally came to a sudden stop in a soft, sticky, stringy type of stuff. For only a few moments everyone was silent. Jimmy noticed that the stuff was wrapped around the force field of his costume. He looked around and said, "Where the heck are we?" "We are stuck!" said Jilly quietly, "we are sticky and we are stuck!" "Well," said Jimmy, "let's try to get unstuck!" "Good idea!" said Fluidica, "but somebody tell me how!"

Just then they heard more strange laughter and from the very top of the cave they saw a dark object coming closer and closer to them. "Children!" laughed the voice, "how I love children!" The sound echoed ever more loudly as a dark feathery creature slid down a thin slimy string of web. "Children of happiness, children of grief, I have you a wish to make or a belief. That can you look at, what can you see? What say you children, what say you three?" "Who are you?" asked Fluidica, "and what do you want with us?" The voice of the creature answered, "The children are fearful, their eyes open wider!

Along on his sticky stuff comes the feared feathered spider! Don't worry little children, I won't do you much harm, I'll be ever so gentle when I rip off your arms!" "We're in trouble now!" said Jilly in a dismal whisper. "Not for long!" said Jimmy struggling, "Not while I have my super powers!" He used all his strength and quickly tore his arms lose from the sticky, stringy spider web. He opened his utility belt and said, "Ok freeze feathery spider, long legs and all!" He held his freeze gun ready to fire.

"Children put away your toys," said the creepy creature. "Now Jimmy, now!" screamed Jilly. With that Jimmy pointed his freeze gun. The monster let out a horrible groan and all of his motion stopped. Jimmy was quick to pull Jilly, her unicorn and her friend, Fluidica, out of the web. "You did it, Jimmy, you did it!" yelled Jilly, so happy that she gave him a great big hug! "Not so fast children," said the feathered spider as he stood motionless. "He talking, it's impossible!" screamed Jilly, "Doesn't the gun work?" "He talking, it's impossible!" screamed Jilly, "Doesn't the gun work?" "Children, this is my domain. This is my home. You can't harm me here!" "He can't catch us if we fly!" said Fluidica. Jimmy shoot him again!" yelled Jilly in a frenzy. Jimmy raised his gun and took careful aim. "I didn't miss this time!" he said confidently. "Let's not play games!" hissed the spider, "come and be my lunch!" "Something's wrong with the gun!" said Jimmy, "it's not working!" "I don't understand!" said Jilly. "Let's get out of here!" screamed Fluidica and she took off. "Wait Flu!" said Jilly, "Wait for us!" "There is no escape!" said the spider still motionless in his same place.

Jilly Applejelly jumped upon her unicorn and flew swiftly away with Jimmy close behind. "I can find you!" echoed the evil voice of the feathered spider, "and when I do, you will be tasty snacks my frightened little children!" Fluidica saw a dim light up ahead and in her squeaky voice said, "Come on guys, let's get out of this cave!" Quickly they flew hoping to leave the cave forever, never to return. "This way!" said Fluidica.

A bright yellow glow filled the inner cave and sparkled more brilliantly than Fluidica's magic dust. "Are you sure this is the way out?" asked Jimmy, somewhat confused. "No," said Fluidica, "but at least it's brighter and we can see where we're going!" "Wow!" exclaimed Jimmy as they approached a glowing section of the cave that was filled to the brim with sparkling jewelry and solid gold coins. "Treasure!" said Jilly. "Ha ha ha", laughed a familiar voice, "you can't escape from me. I found you!" "It's the feather spider!" screamed Jilly. "I don't see him!" said Jimmy anxiously, as a matter of fact, he didn't even follow us when we flew away!" "Then how could he know where we were?" asked Fluidica nervously. "He doesn't!" said Jilly, "it's a trick, like the voices before. It's a dirty rotten trick!!"

"That explains it," said Jimmy, "but who's been playing those tricks on us?" "Who, indeed?" said a voice that echoed in the cool moist cave, "none other than me!" it said. Before them appeared a small dragon about the size of a fox. "Aren't I the greatest?" he said rubbing his knuckles on his scales and steaming his claws with smoke from his nostrils, "I'm the number one best impersonator around."

Jimmy looked at Jilly, at Fluidica and then at the small dragon. "You sure have a big mouth for such a little creature!" he said. "Yeah!" said Fluidica, "and you not only almost caused a fight between us, but nearly scared us to death too!" "Well, I am suppose to protect the treasure," he said, "you're not even suppose to get this far!" "Well, we're here!" said Jilly, "what are you going to do about it?" "I'm going to tell you to get lost!" said the little dragon. "We are lost you dumb dragon!" said Fluidica, "How do we get out of here?"

"Turn around and go back!" said the scaly dragon with the big mouth. "Are you crazy?" asked Jilly, "we were pulled down a tunnel in the cave by a strong forceful wind. "Yeah!" said Fluidica, "we couldn't go back even if we wanted to." "You mean you weren't after the treasure?" asked the dinky dragon. "Of course not!" said Jimmy, "Jilly and Fluidica wanted to explore the cave, not rob it!" "Well, did you find what you were looking for?" asked the small dragon. "The only thing we're looking for is a way

out!" said Jilly.   "The only thing we're looking for now is the exit!" shouted Fluidica.
"I know the exit out of here!" said the dragon, "It's invisible!"

"We could have been trapped in here forever!" exclaimed Jimmy.   "By the way,"
whispered the dragon, shifting his eyes from side to side, as if to see if someone were
watching him.   I'll let each of you take a handful of treasure under one condition."
What's the condition?" asked Jilly in a very low whisper.   "That you never tell a soul
where this treasure came from!" he said.   "We promise," said the trio all at the same
time.   Then they all giggled.   "Shhh!" said the dragon.   "Not so loud, don't make so
much noise!"   "Oh, sorry!" said Fluidica.

Their eyes gleamed as they anxiously stuffed their pockets with polished gold coins and
grabbed hand fulls of diamonds and rubies.   Jilly put on an emerald necklace and helped
Fluidica put on a string of white pearls.   Jimmy opened his utility belt and loaded the
empty spaces with gold and silver coins.   In his pockets he put black and crystal clear
diamonds.   "Don't be so greedy!" said the dragon using Jimmy's mother's voice.
"Don't worry!" said Jimmy, his eyes all a sparkle and his hands grabbing one after
another.

"Wait 'till I go home," said Jimmy to himself.   "I'll be the richest kid on the block.
When I walk down the street people will say, hey, Jimmy gimme some money! I'll say
Ok, why not!"   All of a sudden the cave rumbled, the ground shook and large cracks
formed in the sides of the cave walls.   "Earthquake!" yelled Jimmy.   "Quick, show us
the way out little dragon!" screamed Jilly.   "I forgot which way is out!" he said,

quivering.

The ground shook and a voice echoed throughout the tunnels. It seemed to be calling Jimmy's name. "Cut that out!" said Jimmy to the dragon. "I didn't say anything!" said the dragon. "Jimmy!" called the voice, "Jimmy wake up!" "I am awake!" said Jimmy. "No, you're not!" said the voice as Jimmy felt his body shake back and forth. Jimmy slowly opened his eyes and saw a blurry figure standing over him. "Get up you lazy bum!" said Jimmy's Mother, "your aunt is coming over and I want this house to look clean!" "Ok Mom," he said, with a dry voice that was cracking.

"Where's the treasure!" thought Jimmy to himself, "Where's my super hero costume!" He quickly opened his hands only to find with great disappointment absolutely nothing but air. "Wow," he said angrily, "I could have been the richest guy in town. What happened, where's the money?" He looked under his pillows and pulled the sheet off of his bed. "Jimmy, get dressed and help clean up this house!" said his Mother. "I'm looking for something!" he said loudly. "That can wait!" she said annoyed, "I have something more important for you to do right now!" "Can't it wait?" asked Jimmy hoping he could continue his search. "No, it cannot!" she answered, "hurry up before I get mad!" "Ok," sighed Jimmy, "but I'd rather look for my treasure!" he said quietly to himself. "Where is my superhero costume?" "Clean up your room first and then help me with the dishes!" said his Mother. "Alright Mom!" he said.

"It's genie time," he thought to himself, "Now where did I put that crystal ball."
Jimmy looked into his dresser drawers, into his closet and behind all the boxes of berries.
Under his bed he pulled out a cardboard box marked "Top Secret". "Ahh, there it is!" he
said. He rubbed the crystal ball and the greenish smoke that swirled inside oozed out
into his room. The green genie appeared before Jimmy. "What is it that you would like
me to do for you?" he asked loudly. "Shhh!" hissed Jimmy, "quiet!"

"What are you doing in there?" asked his Mother. "Nothing!" said Jimmy hoping she
wouldn't come in. "Then please be more quiet!" "Ok Mom!" said Jimmy. "What is
it, O' mighty master, what is it that you want?" whispered the genie. "Well, first of
all," said Jimmy, "don't make so much noise when you appear to me! And secondly,
would you do me a favor and clean up this room?" "I hear you and will do as you say!"
said the genie quietly. The strong powerful genie put his hands out and sparks of magic
flew forward. At once Jimmy's room was spotless.

"You know what would be nice?" said Jimmy. "What?" asked the genie in a quiet
whisper. "It would really be nice if I could have that superhero costume!" Jimmy said,
"with a large grin on his face. Jimmy chuckled happily to himself, "And she said I
couldn't do it!" said Jimmy to himself. "What's so funny master?" asked the genie
softly. "Jilly Applejelly said I couldn't be a crime fighter in her world because there
wasn't any crime!" he answered, "but there is plenty here!"

Genie I want my superhero costume and the freeze gun too!" "Granted!" said the genie.
And with that he disappeared. Folded in half on the bed was the superhero costume,
next to it was the freeze gun. "Did you clean up your room Jimmy?" asked his Mother.
"Yes Mom, I did!" he answered. "Already?" asked his Mother. "That's right!" said
Jimmy staring at his superhero costume. "Well, that was fast," she said surprised.
"Come here and help me in the kitchen". Normally Jimmy would have been upset but
now that he had crime fighting on the brain, he didn't mind cleaning up so much.

"I'll be like superman!" said Jimmy to himself, "or better!" First Jimmy helped his
Mother by drying the dishes. Then he swept the small porch. He wiped down the
stove, cabinet shelves, refrigerator, cleaned the tables and took out the trash. "Can I
watch TV now?" he asked. "Not now!" said his Mother, who was now very tired from
mopping and cleaning. "First go to the store for me and when you come back you may
watch television." "But Mom, I'll miss my favorite cartoons!" he complained. "First
the store then the TV!" said his Mother. "Here let me write you a list."

When Jimmy's Mother said the word list, he knew it would be a lot more than five
things to buy. "Oh, no!" said Jimmy to himself, "I'll spend half my day in the store! I
can't even call my genie to go to the store for me!" Jimmy tired and upset took the list
and put it in his shirt pocket. Then went into his room and gazed at his superhero
costume. "I wonder just how shrinkable this thing is?" he thought. He folded it smaller
and smaller and even smaller 'till it was about the size of a stick of gum.

He went in his drawer, took out an old ring box his Mother gave him   and put his

costume inside of it. "You never know when it'll come in handy!" he thought as he

closed his bedroom door and made his way outside. He stuck both of his hands into his

pants pockets and watched his feet as he slowly walked down the street. "I remember

the time my Mother gave me shopping money and on the way to the store I lost it," he

said to himself. Boy, was that a big mistake. I had to go to bed that night without

supper!" "Ha!" he thought, "that was before I found the genie!"

Jimmy carefully waited for the red light to change green and he crossed the street. Near

the store he saw two older kids that looked like they were looking for trouble. Jimmy

wasn't afraid because his superhero costume was in his pocket and if anything happened

he was ready. But even so those guys didn't look like the type you'd like to talk to, so

Jimmy tried to go around them. They blocked his way and he couldn't pass them. So

he turned around and started to walk back home. "Hey shrimp," yelled one of the tough

looking boys. Jimmy kept walking and didn't turn around. "He's talking to you,

midget!" said the other guy.

Jimmy ignored them hoping that he wouldn't have to hurt them. He felt one of the kids

grab his shoulder and pull him around. "Didn't you hear me shrimp!" the tough kid said,

"I was talking to you!" "Look midget, you made my friend angry and that makes me

angry!" said the other kid. "This shrimp is bothering you too Louis?" said the first kid.

"He sure is Jackie!" said Louis. "What do you want to do about it?" "Let's teach him not to be such a trouble maker!" said Jackie. "I'll hold him and you flatten his face."

"No!" said Jimmy. He pulled himself free and ran very fast down the sidewalk. "Get him Jackie!" said Louis. Before Jimmy knew it he felt Jackie's arms wrapped tightly around his legs. His body fell forward and his hands were scrapped from sliding on the rough cement. His chin hit the ground hard. Jimmy struggled to get himself free, but Louis grabbed him under his arms and pulled him to his feet. "I got him!" said Louis proudly. "Now I'm really mad!" said Jackie gritting his teeth, "you're going to pay, shrimp!"

"You touch me and you'll be sorry!" said Jimmy angrily. "Hey, a tough guy!" said Louis keeping a strong hold on Jimmy's arm. "We better not touch him, Jackie! He might hurt us," said Louis chuckling. "You're real funny shrimp," said Jackie, "but as you can see I'm not laughing!" "You going to the store?" asked Louis from behind Jimmy. "Yeah," answered Jimmy while struggling to break lose. "If you were going to the store then you have to have money," said Jackie sneering at Jimmy, "and I want every penney you've got!" "Do you understand you little squirt?"

Jimmy squinched up his eyes and kept his mouth closed. "I asked you a question punk!" yelled Jackie as he leaned forward into Jimmy's face. "Hey!" said Louis, "you're making my friend mad again you ugly midget!" "You know something Louis," said Jackie, "I was going to let this shrimp go but he went on and hurt my feelings!" "What you gonna do?" asked Louis. "Teach him a lesson he'll never forget!" said Jackie with a sour look on his sour face and pushed his knuckles into Jimmy's stomach.

Louis laughed loudly as the tears fell from Jimmy's eyes. "Please don't!" said Jimmy in a whisper. "Don't what?" asked Jackie, "don't do this?" he said as he punched Jimmy hard in the belly. "Where's your money?" asked Louis. "Pocket," said Jimmy in a weak whisper. Jackie reached into Jimmy's back pocket and took the money. "Let's go!" he said to Louis and they both ran off quickly. Jimmy grabbed his stomach, stumbled to the ground and began to cry out loud. He tried to fight the pain and wondered why anyone would want to pick on him.

He reached into the side of his pants pocket and took out one of the magic berries he always carried. The taste of blue berries and cherries went right to work. The pain was gone and Jimmy jumped to his feet. "I'm not going to let you two get away with that!" he said clenching his teeth. He ran into a back alley and took the ring box out of his shirt pocket. He opened the box and quickly unfolded the costume and shook out all the wrinkles. He put on his suit fast and like a flash of lightning he ran down the street after the two tough kids.

Hey Louis, we got almost ten dollars, what do ya say?" "Say hey it's Jimmy Jay," came a voice from a roof top. "Louis you sounded just like that shrimp," said Jackie. "I didn't say that man!" said Louis. Jimmy swiftly flew down behind the two. "Guess who?" he said. They turned about in amazement. "Who are you?" asked Louis. "The guy you beat up, remember?" said Jimmy firmly. "Man, I thought I took care of that dude Louis!" said Jackie. "Yeah, I thought you messed him up good!" Louis said.

"That you did fellows!" said Jimmy snickering, "but I heal fast!" "Will you look at this fool!" said Louis starting to laugh. "Where'd you get the clown suit?" asked Jackie. With that statement Louis spat and sputtered in laughter. "Super fool!" said Jackie, "Super ugly" and super stupid for coming after us!" laughed Louis.

"Want to see something funnier then me?" asked Jimmy. "What could be funnier?" Jackie laughed and slapped Louis' open hands. "Have you two ever looked into a mirror?" asked Jimmy innocently. "Jackie, you know what?" said Louis, "I don't think he learned his lesson, do you?" "I get you Louis, I'll take care of him!" replied Jackie.
    He walked slowly up to Jimmy and grabbed his throat. "You had better learn this time, sucker!" he said.

But before Jackie could blink an eye Jimmy grabbed his collar with two fingers and flung him high up in the air. As he plunged earthward Jimmy quickly took out his freeze gun from the utility belt. "Jackie!" screamed Louis as he saw his friend falling to the hard surface of the ground. Jimmy aimed and fired freezing Jackie's body one foot from the ground. "Ok, you're next!" he shouted at Louis, "it's your turn!" "Hey, hold on man!" said Louis waving his hands. He quickly turned and ran thinking he could out smart Jimmy.

But Jimmy sprang into the air, swooped down and grabbed Louis. "Hey man, let me go!" he said frantically, "I didn't do anything to you!" "Ok," said Jimmy softly, "I'll let you go." He circled back to where he had let Jackie fall and took Louis upward and let him go. "Help me, help me, help me!" shouted Louis as the ground came up fast. Before Louis could catch his breath and yell for help, Jimmy had already flown to the ground. With careful aim he froze Louis also one foot from the ground.

He took his grocery money out of Jackie's pocket and within seconds he swiftly flew back home. He was so very quiet when he came in his Mother never heard him. Silently he snuck into his bedroom. He brought out the crystal ball rubbed it and asked the genie to help him. "Genie I want you to take two bullies and put dresses and lipstick on them! Here's what they look like," he said as he handed the genie the telescope of wonder. "Granted," whispered the genie and disappeared.

Still in his superhero costume, Jimmy made a quiet escape out of his back door. Up into the sky he flew. Greased lightning couldn't have travel faster than the speed he was traveling. One half second later he had arrived to where he had last been. Frozen in time and space were Louis and Jackie. On their faces were frozen expressions of sheer panic. Once wearing shirts and pants, they now wore large fluffy dresses with large red flowers. On their lips shone a bright pink lipstick. Jimmy was so amused by what he had done that tears came out of his twinkling eyes. He laughed so hard that he almost couldn't stop.

"I wish Jilly could see this!" he said as he snickered to himself. He pulled his freeze gun out once more and pointed the round blunt end at the two boys. They came down like two lead balloons and landed with a thud on top of each other. "Ouch! Hey man, get off me with that dress!" said Jackie. "Ooch!" yelled Louis, "my dress, look at yours!" They tried yanking and tugging but the dresses would not come off. They wiped their mouths but the lipstick stuck to their lips!"

"For a couple of tough guys, laughed Jimmy rubbing it in, "you sure look pretty dainty!" "You're going to get it!" shouted Jackie very loudly. "Temper, temper!" said Jimmy wagging his two fingers at them. "Want another flight?" Jackie backed off and said, "Next time, shrimp!" he shook his fist and said, "wait 'till next time!" "Don't dirty your pretty dresses!" said Jimmy mocking the two. Somehow in dresses Louis and Jackie didn't look so tough even if they were.

They walked off in a huff yelling insults at him as they left. Jimmy removed his suit, did his shopping and went straight home. He was very tired. "Jimmy, what ever took you so long?" asked his Mother angrily. "Did you lose the money again?" "Almost Mom, but I found it!" he answered. "Your aunt will be here any minute, help me put away some of these groceries." "Could I take a nap first!" he asked as he began to yawn. "Ok!" said his Mother sympathetically, "you've been very helpful today. I guess a little nap won't do any harm." "Thanks Mom!" said Jimmy, "Boy am I tired!"

He opened the door to his room and staggered over to the bed. He stood at the foot of his bed and let gravity pull him downward. Face down on his bed, there he laid and there he stayed. Two hours later the door bell rang. It was his Aunt Doris. "Jimmy!" yelled his Mother, "Auntie Doris is here!" His Mother and Auntie made their way into his clean bedroom only to find him fast asleep on top of his covers. "Will you look at that!" said Mrs. Jumferjoy, "He must be in dreamland" said his Aunt Doris and they tiptoed out of the room. "We've been looking all over for you Jimmy!" said Jilly, "Where were you?" "Back home," said Jimmy, "fighting crime!" "The dragon told us that there were tunnels in the cave that would have led us to total darkness," said Jilly, lucky we got out!" "Come on Jimmy!" said Jilly, "there's so much more to see!" Fluidica flew up into the air. Jimmy still wearing his super hero costume headed upward after her. Jilly with her flying unicorn flew close behind, over hills and meadows on they went to another exciting adventure.

Chapter 4

JIMMY JUMPFERJOY

AND

MARS BEFORE OUR TIME

It was ten O'clock in the morning when Jimmy awoke, but it looked as though it was five in the morning.

The sky was dark and it was rather cool out. The pitter patter of raindrops danced on the window sills and the distant sounds of thunder echoed for many miles. Lightning flashed quickly on and off as Jimmy rolled out of the soft bed and onto the floor. He climbed to his feet and walked slowly out of his room, still dressed in his play clothes.

"Hey Mom!" He said in his dry waking voice. "Is Auntie Doris still here?"

"No Jimmy, she left very late last night when you were still asleep." Said Jimmy's mother softly. "I'm going out. Do you want anything?"

"No, thank you Mom, but can you drive to the Science Museum?"

"Okay Jimmy," Answered his mother quickly. "Hurry up and get dressed."

Jimmy changed his clothes, cleaned up and left the house to meet his mother in the car.

"where's dad?" asked Jimmy.

"He's out looking for a better job. I hope he finds one Jimmy. Then maybe we can move out of our house. Wouldn't that be wonderful?" She said with a grin.

"You know that big neighborhood with all those fancy houses?"

"Yeah." said Jimmy calmly while watching the windshield
wipers throw the rain water from side to side.

"Well I hope one day soon in my lifetime we could own a
house like that!"

"Don't worry Mom!" said Jimmy confidently. "One of these
days we'll be able to own two or three of them!"

"Oh Jimmy," Laughed his mother, "Keep thinking like that
and maybe we will!" Jimmy smiled at his mother, but inside, his
mind he knew he wasn't joking. Sometime soon he would have his
genie help his parents.

"What's at the science museum Jimmy?" Asked his mother
curiously.

"Oh," He said. "There's a planetarium show about the planet
Mars!"

"What time shall I pick you up?" She asked.

"Well, it's over at around three o'clock." He answered.

"I'll pick you up at four. That will give you time to see
the rest of the museum, okay?"

"Okay," said Jimmy, and he put his arm over his mother's
shoulders.

The wind blew harder, and the rain was coming down so hard
that small floods of water were gushing down the street curbs.

When the old looking car drove up to the Science Museum, the
crooked lightning made the entire sky light up like sunshine.
Three seconds later came the boom of thunder which sounded like
a loud cannon blast.

"I believe I gave you enough money, do you have enough for
lunch?" asked his mother.

"I think so!" said Jimmy.

"Well, have a good time son, see you at four!" She said.

Marcus Bruce

"Okay Mom. See Ya." He said happily. He slammed the car door
and ran up the steps to the Science Museum. He walked inside
and looked around watching the people walking. Slowly, back
and forth, He thought to himself; 'This I know is going to be
fun!' He spend his first few hours looking at the exhibits,
since he had arrived at eleven in the morning. Some were very
large and some small. There was a space area where you could
experience weightlessness on a fake moon surface. In another
area was a large room filled with all types of rocks and gems.
Jimmy looked into one of the windows and saw a rock called
a 'Moonstone'. Just then there was an announcement for the
planetarium show.

"Today you will be able to see mars" said the voice. "Once
said to be the mysterious red planet! When the doors close, no
one will be admitted inside, thank you."

"I'd better hurry," Said Jimmy. "I don't want to miss this
one!" He made his way to the line of people, handed his ticket
to a guard, and went into a room with a big dark structure
in the middle of the floor. The ceiling was dome shaped and
painted white. As the people spoke, their voices were carried
clear over to the other side of the room. The doors closed, the
lights grew very dim, and soft stereo music filled the room.

"Good afternoon," Said a deep voice. "Today our topic is the
red planet Mars. Please do not take any pictures because the
bright flash will only upset other visitors and your film will
be blank. Sit back, relax, as you take a journey to the planet
Mars!"

The music grew louder and a space ship which appeared at the
bottom of the dome led everyone to the planet's surface.

"Mars the planet was named after the god of war!" said a
recorded male voice. "The color of the planet reminded the

ancient people of blood. Toward modern times, people talked
about the possibility of life being on the planet or of
'Martians' digging canals for their water supply. But as we
found from our space probes, there is no life like human life
on that barren red planet.

Jimmy began to slip into a day dream as he watched. 'I
wonder if there really is life on Mars!', he thought. 'I wonder
if I take my magic carpet there will I meet new people or will
I be wasting my time?' The planetarium show soon ended and
the crowd quickly pushed and shoved their way out. One small
boy with a devilish grin put his little foot out in front of
Jimmy's. Poor Jimmy fell right on top of a young girl about his
own age.

"Oh, I'm sorry!" said Jimmy. "It wasn't my fault, a little
brat tripped me!"

"Watch where you are going!" she said sharply. The girl
turned around and faced him. Suddenly Jimmy began to confuse
his words

"Mine sorry, oh, I mean sime sorry, no I mean . . ."

"Never mind what you mean!" said the girl. "Don't do it
again!"

Jimmy couldn't speak straight because he felt a shock
go through him at the sight of the girl. She was the most
beautiful girl he had ever seen. Even prettier than Jilly
Applejelly.

"I won't do it again!" He said. "I promise!"

"Good." said the girl as she began to walk away.

"Hey, wait a minute!" said Jimmy walking after her. "Can I
at least buy you a hot dog?"

"I don't want a hot dog!" said the girl bitterly.

"Well what's your name?" asked Jimmy smiling cheerfully.

Marcus Bruce

"None of your business!" said the girl, "If you don't mind,
I must find my Father!"

"Tina!" said a tall thin man.

"Father!" said the girl.

"where were you? Your mother and I want to leave now!"

"Father, this boy fell right on top of me," she said,
pointing at Jimmy.

"Well never mind," said the man, "We have to go now. Come
on!"

Jimmy was so dazzled by the sight of such a beautiful girl
that he kept trying to figure out why he had to goof up. 'If
only that brat hadn't tripped me, I wouldn't have fallen on
her!' But if I wasn't tripped I never would have noticed her
and she would never have talked to me. She was kind of angry at
me, but I don't care, at least I was able to talk to the most
beautiful girl in the whole world.'

Jimmy couldn't get her wonderful face out of his mind, and
at five minutes to four he was sitting on the stairs in front
of the Science Museum in the rain. He was still thinking to
himself. 'I wonder if I'll ever see her again. And if I do will
she still be angry? What would she do if I suddenly knocked at
her door? Would she frown and tell me to go away? Or invite me
in for popcorn?'

He didn't care that raindrops were soaking his hair and
he didn't notice his mother driving up in their old beat up
used car. 'Maybe I could have the genie bring her to my house
and then I could invite her in for popcorn or something.' He
thought. His mother honked the horn three times before he
realized it was her. He ran down the steps and into the car.

"Did you have fun today?" asked Jimmy's mother.

"Just the best time I've ever had in my whole life." was his answer.

"Did you see any Martians?" she teased.

"What?" asked Jimmy, snapping out of his daze.

"You saw a show on Mars. Did they show any Martians?" she asked.

"No," said Jimmy. "They said there wasn't any life on Mars!"

"Well, what did you see?" she asked.

"Just a lot of stuff," said Jimmy. "But I liked the way they did the stars.

Jimmy and his mother soon arrived home. She fixed him a big meal, and after he had eaten, Jimmy went to his room to play. He closed the door tightly and moved his bed in front of it. Then he went for his crystal ball, rubbed it and out came the genie.

"Yes, oh mighty master." said the powerful genie as the green smoke began to clear. "What is your wish?"

"I'd like to have a mars globe and a toy space ship!"

"Is that all?" asked the strong and powerful genie.

"Wait," said Jimmy. "I've changed my mind!" The genie rolled his large eyes upward.

"I'll call you later, okay?"

"Alright." Said the genie and went back into the crystal ball.

"Tina," whispered Jimmy to himself. "I wonder what Tina is doing?" He went into his closet and pulled out his Telescope of Wonder. "Let me see Tina!" said Jimmy, and immediately, he could see her eating at her dinner table. "Look at the way she eats her food." "Oh, and the way she drinks her juice!" said Jimmy as he stared into his telescope. He watched her leave the dinner table. "Now she's getting up and walking into her

Marcus Bruce

bedroom. She has picked up some clothes and is heading for the bathroom." Jimmy saw her close the bathroom door and turn on the bath water. He pulled the Telescope of Wonder away from his eyes but, then slowly put it back and began to watch again. Tina was preparing to disrobe. She slowly unbuttoned her skirt top and didn't know Jimmy was watching her. This was the first time something like this had happened to Jimmy. He was so shocked he didn't know whether to put down the telescope or keep watching. His heart pounded faster and faster. He could hear it in his ears. Suddenly there was a loud knock at his bedroom door.

"Jimmy!" yelled his mother. Poor Jimmy jerked the telescope from his eyes and in a fit of sheer panic, threw it quickly under his pillows just moments before his mother turned the door knob. He moved the bed from the door and let her in.

"Hi Mom!" Screamed Jimmy and his voice seemed to echo after he was quiet.

"Jimmy, you don't have to shout. I'm not in the kitchen you know!" She said annoyed.

"I'm sorry Mom." He said softly.

"You were so quiet in here that I thought I should check and see if you were alright."

"I'm fine!" said Jimmy holding his heart.

"Well . . . okay," said Mrs. Jumpferjoy, "just checking!"

"Okay," said Jimmy nervously.

She walked out of the room and closed the door. Jimmy let his body go limp and fall backwards onto the bed. He went to reach for the telescope, but remembered that he didn't hear his mother walk away. So he waited until her footsteps went into the kitchen and then went under his pillow to pull out the telescope.

The Amazing Adventures of Jimmy Jumpferjoy

"Now where was I . . ." said Jimmy, eagerly raising the telescope to his eye.

"Jimmy!" yelled his mother, "Jimmy, I forgot to show you what I found."

He threw the telescope so fast under his pillow that his arm hurt and felt his heart pounding in his throat. His mother opened the door and held up a newspaper article she had cut out, in her hand.

"Mom, if you keep doing that I'm going to have a heart attack!" said Jimmy quite nervously.

"What?" she asked.

"Never mind." was his answer.

"Anyway, I thought you'd be interested in this." She handed him the article. The headlines read 'Scientists Claim Ancient Ruins on Mars!' When he saw it he could hardly believe his eyes. In the article, top scientists agreed that they had reason to believe that there were some type of ancient ruins beneath the surface of the red planet due to an unusual find by a Mars probe.

"Ancient ruins!" said Jimmy quietly to himself. "That means there must have been people living there at one time!" His mother smiled and left the room. Jimmy reached for his crystal ball with a brilliant plan bouncing around in his brain.

"Yes, oh mighty master?" asked the genie. "Do you have a wish?"

"I sure do!" said Jimmy pleased with his idea. "Can you turn back the hands of time?"

"Yes, that I can do!" said the genie wondering what Jimmy was going to say next.

"Then when I fly out of the Earth's atmosphere will you send me back before cavemen, before dinosaurs . . . maybe

Marcus Bruce

one billion years before the Earth's surface cooled? And on
returning back, can you bring me back to now?"

"I can and I will if that is your wish." Said the genie

"That's what I want!" said Jimmy.

"It shall be done!" said the genie, and with the last word
spoken the genie vanished. Jimmy decided it would be best to
put another plan to work he went on his journey. He left his
room and said, "What time is it Mom?"

"Eight P.M." said his mother.

"Do you mind if I go to bed early tonight?" He asked.

"I don't mind." She said, "But I hope you'll join your
father and I for supper."

"Okay," said Jimmy. He ate his supper quickly, went into his
bedroom, grabbed his Telescope of Wonder and the Magic Carpet.
Then he tip toed silently out of the house.

"Good night Jimmy!" said his mother sweetly, but he was
already on his Magic Carpet headed for Mars in the night sky.

He had two packets full of magic berries and ate one during
his flight to protect him from any natural harm. He didn't even
need an oxygen mask because the berries took care of him. His
stomach tickled as he glided through space with the greatest
of ease. Soon he was approaching Mars, and could see how much
brighter the stars were here in the blackness of space.

He must have been traveling fast because before long
his journey had ended. He landed in a different time, on a
different planet. The Earth was too far away to see with his
eyes so he used his Telescope of Wonder. It was nothing but
a bubbling, molten round ball glowing like the sun. Mars,
however, was a fresh planet blooming with bright blue grass and
reddish trees. The sky was a purple-blue. The clouds were very
long and fluffy.

"So that's why the planet didn't look red!" he said to himself. Because when Jimmy was still flying towards the planet he noticed the color was different. He had used his Telescope of Wonder and had seen a very large planet in between Mars and Jupiter. It was a bright yellow green and had a large moon nearby. That took Jimmy by surprise, for he had never heard of a planet being there. "This is all very weird!" He said, now sitting on his carpet in a field of orange flowers. "Going back in time changes everything!" The air around him was colder than what he was used to and some of the creatures he saw flying in the air looked odd. This is one weird place!" said Jimmy to himself. He rolled up the carpet and started to walk. He was in a Martian countryside with tall plants around him the size of sunflowers. The further he walked, the more nervous he became. He didn't want to use his magic carpet because he had seen some creatures flying in the air that looked hungry. The trees around were like the giant redwoods, almost as tall as a building. Suddenly there was a low humming type of sound. And he witnessed what looked like a flying saucer zooming across the purple sky. Jimmy scratched his head and kept walking. When his stomach started to grumble he said, "What am I going to do now? How will I know what to eat around here?" Off in the distance he saw a row of great bushes with cherries as large as watermelons. A large smile slowly pushed his cheeks upward. "Just look at the size of those cherries." He said.

"I'm sure I could eat some of those!" He stuck the Telescope of Wonder in between his belt and pants. Then he laid the Magic Carpet on the ground and said, "When I call you, you better come. Don't just sit there if some monster tries to get me!" He pointed his finger at the carpet as if to remind it and made his way to the big green bushes. When he arrived, he

stood before the largest cherries he'd ever seen. Pulling one
of the large fruit from the bush he noticed that it wasn't too
heavy. Jimmy's mouth watered when he smelled it, and after he
bit in the taste was delicious. "Best thing I've ever tasted!"
he said while munching away. "I've never had anything this
good! I don't think." After he finished, he threw away the
seed and went for another one. The red juice from the gigantic
cherry dripped down the sides of his mouth and off his chin. He
cleaned his moist face with his mands, then wiped the wet hands
on his pants. "I'm going to have just one more!" he said, and
reached for another. The red fruit tasted much like cherries
but somehow they were better. The flavor didn't fade away.
Instead, it stayed deep within his mouth.

"Tell me what you are doing?" whispered an unknown voice in
Jimmy's mind. Jimmy looked around quickly and saw no one.

"Who said that?" he said.

"I did." said the strange voice. Jimmy turned completely
around and standing several yards away was a small dark grey
man about four feet tall, floating in the air towards him.
Jimmy backed up in fright.

"What do I do now? Maybe I should call the carpet."

"Don't worry!" said the voice of the stranger.

"Don't do that!" said Jimmy. It feels fully when you talk
inside my mind!"

"It's the only way I know how to talk!" said the strange
grey man.

"My name is Kanue and I've come here to warn you!"

"I'm Jimmy jumpferjoy. Why do you want to warn me? Are these
poison?" He said as he dropped the giant cherry on the ground.

"No!" answered Kanue. "You are in the giant's garden. You
are eating his food!"

The Amazing Adventures of Jimmy Jumpferjoy

"Yipes!" said Jimmy. I don't need any angry giants. I'll just grab a couple of these large cherries and I'll be on my way."

"Are you a traveler?" asked Kanue.

"Yes," said Jimmy. "And I need food because I'm hungry."

Kanue winked one of his very large eyes and said. "Then I shall help you, friend." The two collected two armfuls of those gigantic cherries and started to walk down a pathway. "By the way," said Kanue inside Jimmy's mind. Without warning the ground began to quake and shake. Running toward them was a large grey man ten stories tall.

"Hey!" thundered the giant's loud voice. "Get out of my garden!" Jimmy's heart pounded and sweat formed on his forehead. Kanue was just as frightened. They ran as fast as they could with their arms filled with the giant fruit. "Get out of here you pests!" said the giant angrily.

"Carpet, sweep us off our feet!" said Jimmy. The magic carpet quickly flew past the giant who was waving his hands in the air trying to smack it down.

"Get out of here!" wailed the giant. Go on you pests get out!"

Jimmy's carpet swiftly and easily moved like the wind far from the giant and his bigger than truck hands.

"Those silly little people!" laughed the giant as they flew out of sight. "They're always coming into my garden!

It makes me want to laugh every time I see them move their tiny little feet!" The giant smiled to himself and walked back home. "Those funny little people." He chuckled.

Meanwhile Jimmy and Kanue wiped the sweat off of their foreheads. They were frightened very badly.

"Where are we going?" asked Kanue.

Marcus Bruce

"I don't know!" said Jimmy. Why don't you tell me where we should go!"

"We'll go to the land of Staycons." Said kanue. "I'll introduce you to the twins!"

"What twins?" asked Jimmy.

"Bin and Ban!" said kanue.

"Are they important?" asked Jimmy.

"No," said kanue. But they're my friends."

"By the way," asked Jimmy curiously. "How old are you?"

"How old do I look?" asked Kanue.

"I don't know, about twenty-five or twenty-six?" said Jimmy.

"I'm about six million years old!"

"That's probably because you're a Martian!" said Jimmy.

"What's a Martian? Asked Kanue.

"You are." Said Jimmy, "You're from planet Mars aren't you?

"We call this planet Monogomora." said Kanue. There is a planet not far from here still forming, we will name it Soil."

"I call it Earth!" said Jimmy.

"Same thing!" said kanue.

They flew out of the Martian countryside into the Martian city; a wonderfully beautiful place with many different flying saucers, all shapes and sizes. One huge space ship that looked like a flying bus passed by the Magic Carpet very slowly.

"You see that big round dome down there?" asked Kanue.

"Yeah," said Jimmy.

"That's where Bin and ban live." said Kanue.

"Will they let me ride in a flying saucer?" asked Jimmy hoping to get a positive answer.

"What's a flying saucer?" asked Kanue.

"You know!" said Jimmy. "Those round space ships that look like giant plates."

"What are plates?" asked Kanue.

"Oh, forget it!" said Jimmy angrily.

"If you're talking about those airborne vehicles; we call them sils. They are powered by hydroelectric and solar energy, reaching speeds up to six zillion miles faster than the speed of light."

"Wow!" said Jimmy. "Can I go on one?"

"No, not today." said Kanue. "Perhaps some other time."

When the carpet landed, they were greeted by two young twins, having grey skin like Kanue. Their eyes were very large and long.

"Hello," said Bin in a friendly tone of voice.

"Hi!" answered Ban.

"I'm not talking to you!" said Bin. "I'm speaking to Kanue.

"Kanue who?" asked Ban.

"You know Kanue and he knows you too." answered Bin.

"I know Kanue?" asked Ban

"Sure you do, you know Kanue!" said Bin.

"I know Kanue, really I do?" asked Ban.

"Sure you do you flip flop fool!" said Bin. "I know Kanue, you know Kanue, everybody knows Kanue!"

"Well, why didn't you say so?" said Bin.

"What did you say?" asked Ban.

"I said!" answered Bin closing his fingers in a tight fist. "You know Kanue!"

"Kanue who?" asked Ban.

"Here we go again!" said Bin. "Please forgive my brother he's not too bright."

"Well," said Kanue. "I brought you a traveler. His name is Jimmy Jumpferjoy.

"Where are you from, Jimmy?" asked Kanue.

"Earth!" said Jimmy.

"But the planet Soil hasn't even formed yet!" said kanue in a confused manner.

"You're not a time traveler, are you?" he asked.

"Not really." said Jimmy.

"I didn't think so." said Kanue.

"Can I ask a question?" asked Jimmy.

"Go ahead." said Kanue.

"Um, how come no one moves their lips around here?" asked Jimmy pointing to his mouth. Ban looked at his brother, at Kanue and then at Jimmy. "How come?" He asked. "Well maybe I'm jealous." Said Jimmy quickly, shrugging his shoulders.

"Now then Bin and Ban, since you're the official Staycon tour guides," said Kanue. "I would like you to show our young guest this city and others he might be interested in on the big screen.!"

"Sure thing." said Bin. "Come on Ban!"

They entered the dome structure and went down deep into a tunnel.

"Underneath," said Bin. "We have a city under construction in case of emergency!"

"That's right!" said Ban. "Last season, about five hundred years ago, we were attacked by the evil Cramanians!"

"Who are they?" asked Jimmy curiously.

"You don't know about the Cramanians?" asked Bin.

"They are the worst. The meanest, the ugliest things in the whole galaxy." answered Ban.

"And if you are not careful Jimmy, you can become one!" said Bin.

"How?" asked Jimmy. "Is it like having a disease?"

"Well," said Ban. "Did you ever know anybody that was always nice and friendly?"

"Yeah," said Jimmy.

"They were always happy and you liked them a lot?" asked Bin.

"Yeah," said Jimmy.

"Did your friend ever stop being friendly and nice, instead they began to act mean and evil?" asked Ban.

"Well," said Jimmy.

"Did you ever look in their eyes and see a different person?" asked Bin.

"No!" said Jimmy.

"When they smiled did it look like they weren't happy, and they acted as cold as ice to you?" asked Bin.

"Yeah," said Jimmy.

"Then they became a Cramanian!" said Ban.

"Yeah, and you can always tell a Cramanian by their ice cold eyes!" said Bin.

"And the way that they all of a sudden cause trouble, trying to make you do the same." said Ban.

"How does that happen?" Jimmy asked, trying to figure out how to avoid becoming a Cramanian.

"Have you ever become sick with the flu?" asked Bin.

"A long time ago, I used to get sick." said Jimmy.

"The Cramania bug or organism is not visible to the eye, so our scientists have a laser type microscope able to see even the tiniest of things." Said Bin as Ban nodded his head up and down. "The scientists have seen it get into the body traveling up to the brain? After that happens, the nice person you once knew becomes evil and grouchy." said Bin.

Marcus Bruce

"But." said Ban. "There is a cure, the elemental organism!
It fights hard and strong till the Cranania organism leaves."

They walked down a long grey corridor and entered a large
room with hundreds and thousands of seats. In the very front of
the room was a very large screen with rounded corners.

"What city would like to see first Jimmy?" asked Bin.

"How about this city?" He said.

"Very well," said Ban. "Here we go!" Bin and Ban showed
Jimmy every section of the city good parts and bad. They also
showed him the area where they made their space vehicles; which
Jimmy was very interested in.

"Can I take a flight?" asked Jimmy hopefully. "I've never
been in a UFO before."

"I'm sorry, we can not do that!" said Bin.

"Oh, please!" said Jimmy anxiously. "Please can I ride in
the flying saucer?!"

"Sorry I'm afraid that no aliens can ride in our sils!" said
Bin.

"I know what. I'll show you my Telescope of Wonder!" said
Jimmy, hoping this would help. "You can see anyone, anywhere
and I mean anywhere!"

"Hey Bin," said Ban. "Maybe you don't want to help him, but
I do!"

"Alright!" said Jimmy. "First I get to ride!"

"No!" said Ban. "First we get to see the telescope."

"Well, okay," said Jimmy. "You win. But you had better keep
your promise." He handed Ban the telescope and told him how to
work it. Ban wanted to see where the Cramanians were and to his
surprise it looked like they were headed for the city.

"We'd better sound the alarm Bin. The Cramanians are coming,
millions of them!"

The Amazing Adventures of Jimmy Jumpferjoy

"Where are they?!" asked Bin, fearing that they would
undergo another attack on their city.

"I don't know!" said Ban pacing back and forth nervously.

"Quick. Let me see that thing!" said Bin angrily as he
jerked the telescope away from his brother. He looked into
the telescope and asked to see the location of the Cramanian
ships, only to find that they were six galaxies away in another
dimension. "Ban!" said Bin. "They are not even close by, you
idiot!"

"But they looked so close, you bug-eyed beetle." said Ban.

"Don't call me a bug eyed beetle you pug-nose gloata!" said
Ban.

"You're a pug-nose gloata, and you smell like one too!'

"What?" said Bin.

"You not only look and smell like a pug-nose gloata,
but you've got floggoes up your suit and your mother eats
pielows.!"

"Your mother eats pielows too!" said Ban. "Because your
mother is my mother!"

"Does she really eat pielows?" asked Bin.

"I don't know," answered Ban.

"You said I could ride in a UFO remember?" said Jimmy
painfully

"That's right. We did!" said Bin. "Let's go."

They took Jimmy to the base, where Jimmy saw over one
billion space ships on short cylinders. They pushed a button
and energy packs appeared at the back of their silver colored
space suits. They lifted Jimmy up and glided him to a bright
florescent blue round space ship. A slit appeared in the space
ship and they went inside. While inside, Jimmy could see

various small bright lights in many different colors. They
reminded Jimmy of Christmas lights in small rows of three.

   Two or three bright strobe lights flashed in a pattern
above his head and to the left and right were smaller versions
of the big screen he had seen earlier. He walked over to one
of the screens and the pictures on it seemed to be standing
outside. They were so real looking, Jimmy reached out to touch
the pictures but his hands went through it. The screen showed
a long cigar shaped ship, longer than the one he was on, float
by slowly and let out three smaller space ships which zipped
off in different directions. On the other screen he could see
a ship coming out of hyperspace. It fluttered up and down very
quickly like humming birds wings and reminded Jimmy of the
times he had waved his fingers in front of the T.V. screen at
home. Just then a man darker grey than the twins came in and
they spoke to him in their own language.

   "Mazno tan go zie boatie lank mebez!" said Ban.

   "Merko larz piter Kaneo lapid terwa." said Bin.

   "Bees lika fando zam xando ipsod fezto redta marzo" answered
the darker grey man. He turned and left.

   "What happened? asked Jimmy wondering.

   "We had to explain that you were a friend of ours." said
Bin.

   "Yeah," said Ban. "He didn't think we should give you a
ride."

   "Why not?" asked Jimmy.

   "Because you are an alien!" answered Bin.

   "Here comes the doctor." said Ban.

   "I don't need a doctor!' said Jimmy.

   "Everyone is checked!" said Bin. "Especially aliens!"

The doctor placed Jimmy's hands on an ice cold metal block. Touched him on the forehead, squeezed both of his arms, and handed him two pills. He turned to Bin and Ban speaking in their own language "Zivo paton whyzon cano cievaia!" he said.

Bin and Ban explained to Jimmy that the doctor advised them not to take him on a flight unless he's taken the two pills and rested at least three or four days.

"I don't need medicine!" said Jimmy. "I have my Magic Berries!"

"What's that?" asked Ban.

"They keep me well no matter what." Jimmy handed two berries to the doctor and let him examine them. He came back amazed and said. "Lay fo tomwie!"

"Doctor says it's okay!" said Bin

"Really?" asked Jimmy. "Well can I go now?"

Ban nodded his head up and down and the doctor left the room staring at the berries, scratching his head.

"Now take a seat and we will take you on a trip around the universe, okay?" said Bin.

"Great!" Said Jimmy. "I don't believe it. This is excellent!"

"Did you notice the buttons on the ship?" asked Bin.

"Yeah," said Jimmy. "They look like three dots in a pyramid shape."

"We call it triple dots," said Bin. "They can be found in absolutely every part of the galaxy in every solar system, every universe and all worlds. You even have triple dots on your face."

"Where?" asked Jimmy, somewhat confused at what he had just heard.

"Your two eyes and your nose make triple dots!" said Ban.
"When you look up into the night sky and see the brilliant
stars, you can easily see the brilliant stars, you can easily
pick out the triple dots!" said Bin. "They're everywhere!"

"I'll keep that in mind." said Jimmy. "But when can I have
my ride?"

"In a minute," said Bin. "Take a seat anywhere you like, but
sit by one of the screens." said Ban.

"There are two screens." said Jimmy."

"Hurry it up!" said Bin. "When I touch this flashing orange
light we will be on our journey.

"Slick and a half!!" said Jimmy clinging on to his Magic
Carpet, which was rolled up under his arm, and took a seat.

Bin touched the flashing orange light. A humming sound went
from very low to a very high pitch, the lights spun around
the room slowly at first, then quickly picked up speed. Jimmy
closed his eyes just for a second. When he opened them she saw
Jupiter wiz by.

They went past Saturn next, at a fantastic rate of speed.
After they passed Pluto, they entered a new galaxy and kept
going. Jimmy's eyes opened wider as they passed asteroid belts,
comets and black holes. Once in a while, they could see other
UFO's going in another direction, looking like nothing more
than a blur. They flew by whole solar systems, some with ten
planets, others with only three; some with one or two suns,
into and beyond supernovas. Jimmy noticed a black hole that
the ship was approaching, and was very worried the ship would
be sucked in. Then, in moments, his worst fear came true. The
ship went directly into the black hole. All around him he
could see streams of light disappear into the opening. Whole
meteorites came inside rotating slowly into a black mass of

nothingness. Within microseconds, the space ship came back out with everything else that was sucked into the hole. Bin touched a bright green flickering button and the lights on the ship reversed. The ship moved even faster. The stars disappeared and sparks of light were flashing on and off like lightning streaks, quickly bouncing off one another. Small bright explosions happened soon afterwards. Bin touched a dull red button. Suddenly the whole ship wavered from side to side. It moved so fast that it seemed they were inside a hummingbird's wing during flight. Jimmy then saw Mars on the screen, coming up very fast. The high pitch sound was herd then it went to a very low hum, the lights stopped rotating around, and the next thing he knew he was back where they had started.

"That was quick!" said Jimmy.

"We didn't want to alarm you," said Ban. "So we took the slowest sil."

"Can I have another ride?" asked Jimmy.

"No," said Bin. "But I hope you enjoyed this one!"

"Slick and a half!" said Jimmy.

"Kanaue will take you to the nutrition utarium." said Bin.

"What's that?" asked Jimmy.

"A fast food place!" said Bin.

Kanue came by with a very small vehicle like the one Jimmy had the ride on but only about four people could fit inside. He took Jimmy non-stop to the fast food district. The utarium was a square shaped building made of polished metal. Inside there were horrible odors that would make a grown man cry.

"Try one of these!" said Kanue as he handed Jimmy a round thing that looked like an oatmeal cookie.

"Sure," said Jimmy, and he eagerly stuffed the cookie into his mouth. "Well, what do you think?" asked Kanue. Jimmy looked as though he had just eaten a lemon rind. He squinched up his face and wrinkled his nose.

"Yuck!" said Jimmy as he spit it out of his mouth into his hand. "This stuff is awful! It tastes exactly like cardboard!"

"What's cardboard?" asked Kanue. "And how long have you been eating cardboard!"

"That's only an expression," said Jimmy angrily still spitting out what was left.

"What's an expression?" asked Kanue.

"Forget it." Said Jimmy, and they did.

"Well, I think I'd better be going now." Said Jimmy after a while becoming bored with the place.

"Have you seen the park?" asked Kanue.

"Why. What's the park?" asked Jimmy.

"It's a place where a great wizard appeared one day. He was a special man with many wise things to say."

"What did he talk about?" asked Jimmy in a curious manner.

"For one thing, he thanked us for keeping peace in the galaxy and told us that when Soil becomes a planet, we should go there to fight the Cramanians."

"Some how this man sounds familiar. What was his name?" asked Jimmy.

"His name, I believe was Saysoo." said Kanue looking skyward. "He was traveling with two other travelers which had a bright glow about them. A friend of mine took a three dimensional picture which hangs on a tree in the park." said Kanue, thinking back to the past."

"The name doesn't sound right, but it sounds like you're talking about something religious." said Jimmy.

"What's religious?" asked Kanue.

"Forget it!" said Jimmy.

"Then come with me," said Kanue.

They walked to the park and there on an enormous redwood-like tree was a huge picture of a man.

"Wow!" said Jimmy. "That's the biggest picture I've ever seen." When he walked form one side to the other, he could almost see all sides of the man. The face of the man looked familiar but he had grey skin and his eyes were as large as everyone else on the planet. "I've seen that face before!" said Jimmy. "But I don't know where!" Suddenly, from out of the purple sky, appeared thousands upon thousands of dark green space vehicles.

"Cramanians!" yelled Kanue. "They're here!" The alarm sounded throughout the entire city. Jimmy panicked and didn't know what to do. He reached for Kanue's hand, but Kanue ran for help in another direction.

"Wait Kanue! Wait Kanue!" screamed Jimmy. He started to run after Kanue and couldn't keep up. He sat on the ground. Carpet rolled up under his arm and telescope under his belt. "What the heck do I do now?"

As the Cramanians moved in closer, Jimmy got up and ran several yards towards the park. Then he looked around in confusion for a place to hide. He ran to the left and then to the right. "Where am I going?" he asked himself. "Stay cool Jimmy!" he said, as the sound of thousands upon thousands of space ships approached. "Don't loose your head now!" He looked upward in time to see bright white hot rays shooting downward in a straight line, and striking the ground. "That's the Staycon city!" said Jimmy to himself. The bright rays were flickering and flashing one after another, like the ending of a fireworks display. When they hit the ground, Jimmy could hear explosions off in the distance. Seconds later the Staycon

Marcus Bruce

city fired back. A bright rainbow colored ray came up from the
ground and hit some Cramanian space ships, while others fired
back. "This is like a nightmare!" yelled Jimmy grabbing his
face. "How do I get out of here?" Just then, Jimmy noticed an
old tree with a very large hole down at the base of the tree.
"Maybe I can hide inside here!" he said to himself. He stuffed
his carpet into the hole and climbed into it himself. "Where's
my stupid genie when I need him!" he said under his breath.
As the ships came closer, Jimmy could smell the clean air
turning smoky and sour. Through the hole in the large tree he
noticed that off in the distance the Staycon city had put up a
repellant force field. Rays were bouncing off it like sparks.
"I knew I forgot something. I should have brought my super hero
costume!" said Jimmy. A bright flash made his eyes blink, for
a ray had hit the ground right in front of the tree. In less
than a half second, the ground became liquid and rehardened
just as fast. Then another and another, the rays were coming
down like rain. Soon the ground was filled with holes. Jimmy
stuck his head out to see if the Cramanians had gone, when
all of a sudden a blinding light flashed five inches from his
nose. It struck the root of the tree and a fire started. Jimmy
could smell something burning and he could hear the crackle
of flames. It was then that he realized he couldn't see. "I'm
blind," yelled Jimmy. "I can't see!" he put out his hands
trying to find his Magic Carpet as the flames danced up the
tree. "Help!" he yelled, "Won't somebody help me!" Tears found
their way down his face as he screamed. "Kanue, anybody, help
me, I'm blind. I should never have come here!" he cried. "How
will I ever survive this?" He walked out of the tree still
unable to use his sight, clutching his Magic Carpet.

He stumbled about feeling the heat of other near misses by the powerfully destructive rays. As he rolled the Magic Carpet out on the ground, once very smooth, now filled with crater-like holes, He felt the heat of another ray, but this one landed right on his leg. Jimmy screamed in pain. The section where the ray hit started to melt away. He fell to the ground and grabbed a hold of the leg that was almost completely melted away. No longer fighting his tear, he cried out in extreme pain. "G-Go carpet!" he stuttered. "Please t-take me back home!" His voice ended in a squeaky tone. "I haven't felt this b-bad since the time a car . . ." Suddenly he remembered the magic berries. He reached into his pocket. "These better work!" he said, with misty eyes. His hands went in his pocket, the berries went into his mouth and worked within seconds. Soon after he swallowed the juice, his eyesight returned, he was able to watch his leg heal right before his eyes. Since his command had brought Jimmy into the air, he flew high above the wreckage and could see that much of the whole planet had been destroyed by the raid. The plants and trees were burnt. The sky began to look different and Mars looked like a dying planet. When the carpet flew Jimmy out into space, he noticed that the planet between Mars and Jupiter had been totally destroyed. Only pieces of the planet remained in orbit. "Wow!" said Jimmy. "I know what happens now. The whole planet becomes a desert. Probably after another attack by the Cramanians. It turns into nothing but a big red dusty planet!" When Jimmy returned home in his own time period, he tip toed silently into the house.

"Jimmy!" said his mother, creeping up behind him. "What are you doing up?"

"I, um," said Jimmy in a moment of shock. "Well you see, um, I um."

Marcus Bruce

"Do you realize its nine-thirty you only slept for an hour!"
she said.

"It's only been an hour?" said Jimmy. "But it seemed like a
whole day! I thought I had been gone for a long time!"

"You didn't go anywhere, you went to bed after supper,
remember?" she said. But Jimmy remembered sneaking out and
taking his carpet to Mars before our time. Maybe if he told his
mother it was a dream he could tell her the whole story.

"Mom, I know what happened to Mars!" he said. "There was
a kind of war and much of the land was turned to waste on the
surface!"

"What an imagination!" laughed his mother. "Perhaps you
should go to bed, finish your dream and see what happens next,
okay?" She said. Looking at Jimmy she shook her head. "Do me
a favor, wear your clean pajamas to bed, take off your play
clothes, and leave rugs on the floor where they belong!"

Jimmy looked at the Magic Carpet rolled up under his arm and
at his clothes, dusty and dirty from being on Mars. He washed
up, put his pajamas on and climbed into bed. "One of these days
I'm going to meet them again!" said Jimmy with covers up to
his chin. "I'll bet any money those guys can time travel!" He
yawned, his eyes closed ever so slowly and you could hear him
say something about Jilly Applejelly as he talked in his sleep.

END

Chapter 5

JIMMY JUMPFERJOY

AND

THE VALLEY OF THE DEAMONS

Six weeks passed. Jimmy Jumpferjoy was doing so much traveling here and there, that he decided to take a vest for a while and play at home. He called up his best friend Joey who had a lot to tell him.

"Jimmy," said Joey over the phone. "I was over by Tompsons strange and unusual gift shop and I found the weirdest thing floating down the street. Meet me at the playground and I'll tell you about it!"

"Okay, said Jimmy." And he met Joey at the swings in the playground. "What's happening?" asked Jimmy.

"This old piece of paper I found. Read it!" said Joey. Jimmy read the strange, yellowish wrinkled up paper. "In case you don't know the time is right. Yes the time is right. From now on, whatever happens, it will always turn out for the better. So don't fret and don't worry. Try to have as many good dreams as possible, because whether you like it or not, your dreams or at least most of your dreams will come true. So hang on to your head, get up and dance, because you, yes you, can have one but only one wish granted. If perhaps nothing happens, consult your local Leprechaun and if you haven't one then go with me. If you do go to me beware of the many dangers of surrounding obstacles. Dive head first into fantasy and you will arrive at my door. For good luck along the way, close your eyes and count to three, or say the alpabet backwards. Maybe even clap your hands three times and touch each shoe. By the way, as long as you are on your journey to me, no bad luck or ill favors will befall you. Ask for guidance and you will receive it. Starting out is the hard part, however, if you like me, I'll like you all the more for it. With promisig holes in the sky, you should see the rainbow mountains, continue westward. Until you reach the land of the seting sun. There you will find happiness, joy and all the good things that follow. But take advantage of the things that happen without concern. With all these signs, you should find many exciting things to see. Many of which are strange and unknown. Wherever you go, you will run into the color red. In the clouds, the dirt, everywhere. Then when you least expect it, everything red will turn blue. From blue to green, green to yellow, and back to red.

You will meet many new and wonderful people. If anything should go wrong, close your eyes as tight as you can, say the alphabet backwards and the gloom will pass away. Find many new friendships and you will have more friends than you can count. Finally, you should reach me after this fanciful journey and it will be worth every moment of it. If Kagina knew Kanue, why don't you know Kanue too!"

"What does it mean?" joey asked Jimmy.

"You know that part where it says why don't you know Kanue?" asked Jimmy.

"Yeah?" said Joey.

"Well, don't tell anyone, but I met him!" said Jimmy in a low whisper.

"You did really?" asked Joey.

"Yeah!" said Jimmy. "He's from Mars."

"Mars!" screamed Joey loudly. "You're lying!"

"Shhh!" said Jimmy with his finger covering his lips. "Lets go back to the gift shop and see what else we can find!"

Marcus Bruce

"Alright," said Joey. "Come on."

They left the playground and went to tompsons gift shop.
There were other papers that joey had not picked up.

"Supernatural magic," read Jimmy as he picked up a paper. "I
wonder what this one is about."

"Read it." Said Joey.

"Well it says here 'LESSON ONE: Learning to Zap.'" Said
Jimmy. And he read on.

"Here's how to zap; think about energy lightning and all the
powers of the universe. Then think about your victim. Imagaine
that they are much weaker than you. Then strike by piercing
their eyes with yours."

"What else does it say?" asked Joey.

"LESSON TWO:," said Jimmy. "To help you in your practices.
You should mix up a secret formula. Take two teaspoons of
baking soda, not baking power and mix it into a tall glass of
spring water. Then add two to three teaspoons of sugar and
mix."

"What do you do then?" asked Joey.

"Drink the whole mixture." Said Jimmy. "It may taste bad,
you may even want to throw it out but don't. LESSON THREE:,"
said Jimmy still reading." The Art of Getting the Things you
want. But before you read any further, you know you have no
business being so greedy. After all Jimmyjumpferjoy, you have
the crystal ball!"

"What?" said Joey. "What are you talking about?"

"Wait Joey. Let me finish reading this." Said Jimmy as he
read aloud once more. "you had better let go of this paper
unless you want roasted fingers!" Jimmy immediately dropped the
paper and it burst into flames.

The Amazing Adventures of Jimmy Jumpferjoy

"Did you see that Jimmy? The paper caught fire all by itself." Said Joey. "Let's get out of here!" They both turned and ran. Joey went to his house and when Jimmy came home he slammed the door behind him. His heart pounded like a drum, faster than he could ever remember.

"Jimmy, please do not slam the door when you come in!" said Mr. Jumpferjoy sternly.

"Um okay Dad." Said Jimmy nervously. Somehow he had the weird feeling that someone or something was watching him right in his own home.

In the corner of his eye he saw something run quickly into the bathroom. He tuned around and slwoly walked into the bathroom. He checked behind the shower curtain and found nothing. He scratched his head when he felt something touch his shoulder. "Yipes!" he said and quickly jerked around, but nothing was there. "Wonder what's going on?" he asked himself. His eyes slowly shifting from left to right. "Maybe it would be better if I stay in my room." He said. But something quickly flew out of his room and went quickly into another room. "I saw that!" he said to himself, and as he went after it, the telephone rang. Jimmy picked up the telephone and answered it. "Hello?" he said. A loud, evil laugh came over the phone, then click, they hung up.

"Who was it?" asked Jimmy's father.

"I don't know!" said Jimmy feeling nervous. "They laughed, then just hung up!"

"Probably some kids playing with the phone!" said Mr. Jumpferjoy.

"I certainly hope so!" said Jimmy. He wanted to be sure Joey was all right, so he quickly dialed the numbers on the phone.

"Who is it?" came a strange voice.

Marcus Bruce

"Is Joey home?" he asked.

"I'm sorry said the voice on the phone. Joey died this morning!"

"No!" said Jimmy very upset. "That can't be. I saw him this morning!"

"Well, he must have died shortly afterwards." Said the voice. "You better pray that you're not next." The stranger's voice started to laugh louder and louder 'till Jimmy hung up.

"I don't know what's going on, but I don't like it!" he said nevously to himself. Suddenly there was a knock at the door. "Um Dad? I think it's for you" said Jimmy to his father.

"I'm too busy Jimmy, please get it for me, would you?" said his father. Not knowing what to expect, he slowly and cautiously approached the front door. In his mind he pictured some type of hariy monster grabbing him by the throat and tossing him on to the cement. The knock at the door grew louder, thump, thump, thump. Like a creature with hard crusty green knuckles. Jimmy could feel his hands shake, his throat went dry and the beating of his heart pounded in his ears like the knock at the door.

"Um, how come I have to answer the door.?" Asked Jimmy.

"I told you son, I'm busy right now" said Mr. Jumpferjoy in another room. Why don't you come here and help me ?!" said Jimmy nervously putting his fingers into his mouth.

"Don't be funny! You open that door and find out who's there young man!" said his father in an angry tone of voice. The knocking came faster as if someone were in trouble. This made poor Jimmy even more nervous.

"Who is it?" he asked. But there came no answer. The knocking stoped. Jimmy turned away feeling relieved and took a deep, deep breath. Then the knocks continued. He didn't want

to, but Jimmy walked back over to the door know and suddenly
flet ants crawling up and down his face. When he opened the
door, the feeling went away. `

Standing in the doorway was Joey. "Help!" screamed Jimmy
frantically. "Dad, help!"

He slammed the door hard, and ran to his worried father.

"What's the matter son?" asked Mr. Jumpferjoy.

"A ghost!" yelled Jimmy. "There's a ghost outside.

"What are you talking about?" said his father. "There's no
such thing."

"L-look on the s-steps!" stuttered Jimmy. His father opened
the ddor and saw little Joey jast as nervous as Jimmy was.

"Come in Joey!" said Mr. Jumpferjoy.

"No!" screamed Jimmy, backing up into a corner of the room.
"Get him out of here. he's dead!"

"Don't be funny Jimmy!" said Mr. Jumpferjoy. "I don't think
he's feeling too good today Joey. He's been acting strange all
morning."

"That's okay." Said Joey. "I'm not dead Jimmy, really."

"But your mother said . . ." began Jimmy.

"What do you mean my mother said? My mother is in New York
visiting her sister."

"But when I called your house, soneone said that you died!"

"Probably a wrong number." Said Mr Jumpferjoy leaving the
room.

"Joey, I'm worried!" Jimmy said patting his frined on the
back. "Something's happening and it's making me go haywire!"

"That's why I came over here." Said Joey. "Something's
running around in my house but never really can see what it
is!"

Marcus Bruce

"It kind of flies by the corner of your eye, right?" said Jimmy.

"Right!" said Joey. Just then Jimmy heard a buzzing in his ears.

"Listen Joey, do you hear that?"

"What?" asked Joey.

"That buzzing sould, it sounds like bees!" answered Jimmy.

"I think it would be a good time to try that magic formula!" said Joey.

"Yeah!" said Jimmy.

They both walked into the kitchen but when they did, they felt like spider webs were on their faces. They wiped at their faces and looked at one another. Jimmy poured a glass of water and heard someone call his name in a very raspy voice.

"What?" he asked.

"Nothing!" said Joey.

"Didn't you call me Joey?" he asked.

"Call you what?" asked Joey.

"Nevermind!" said Jimmy. "I forgot how much sugar we mix."

"Something like two or three teaspoons." Said Joey.

"How much baking soda?" asked Jimmy.

"Only two teaspoons!" said Joey. Jimmy stirred the baking soda and sugar 'till it was clear. He handed the formula to Joey.

"You go first." He said.

"Not me, you!" said Joey.

After the drink was passed from Joey to Jimmy, back to Joey again, something flew into the room and went behind the stove.

"He's in the room!" Said Jimmy. "Give me the drink!"

"Me first!" said Joey

"No me!" said Jimmy.

"Joey grabbed the tall glass and took a drink. He frowned
a terrble frown and began to cough. He put the drink down.
Took a deep breath and as chills went up his back he swallowed
the last gulp quickly. Shaking heis head from side to side he
blew air through his lips. "Yuck!" he said. I hope this stuff
works!"

"Hey, you didn't leave any any for me!" said Jimmy.

A strong gust of wind blew into the room. The curtains in
the kitchen, flapped up and down. The glass fell over, rolled
across the table and fell to the ground with a loud crash.

"What was that?!" yelled Jimmy's father.

"A glass fell down!" said Jimmy.

"Well, clean it up!" said his father. "And make sure you get
up all those little pieces too, okay?"

"Alright," said Jimmy. "Joey, help me clean up this mess!"
They took the broom and dust pan out then swept up the broken
glass. The big pieces went into the trash bag. They wet a
tissue and wiped the floor for the small, unseen particles of
glass. "You know what joey . . ." Jimmy stopped in mid sentence
for just then, in the kitchen on the wall, he saw a dark shadow
moving slowly across it. The shadow was directly behind Joey
and Jimmy stared at it but Joey thought Jimmy was looking at
him.

'What's wrong?" asked Joey. As the shadow came off the wall
and floated towards him.

"Look out!" shouted Jimmy. Joey took a dive to the floor and
the shadow flew out of the window.

"What was it?" asked Joey.

"I don't know. Something dark and it came off the wall after
you!" Said Jimmy anxiously.

Marcus Bruce

"Jimmy, what we need is one of those people who get rid of ghosts." Joey said.

"Maybe we can find one in the phone directory!" Jimmy answered. "Hey Dad, where's the Yellow Pages? Mr. Jumpferjoy did not answer. "Hey Dad, I said where are the Yellow Pages?" asked Jimmy again.

"I don't think your dad is home any more." Said Joey quietly.

"He wouldn't leave us here all alone!" said Jimmy. "Not my dad anyway!"

"He didn't know anything was going on!" said Joey

"But he can always tell when I'm scared!" said Jimmy. "Just like when he knows I'm lying!"

"Maybe the shadow got him!" said Joey looking from side to side.

"Maybe not!" said Jimmy angrily, hoping his friend would be wrong. "Is anybody home? Dad?" He looked into his father's room finding no one there. He knocked on the bathroom door and when no one answered, he looked inside. He looked carefully in the basement. Joey helped him look outside to see if he was anywhere near the house. "He's got to be somewhere!" said Jimmy feeling his stomach begin to get upset.

"Maybe he was turned into a housefly by some kind of witch!" said Joey. Or maybe he wasn't!" said Jimmy angrily. "Joey!! How would you like it if I told you that your mother or father were changed into something?!"

"Wouldn't bother me!" said Joey.

"Well it bothers me!" said Jimmy. Suddenly they heard the wooden floor creek in Jimmy's bedroom. "Yiper Ciper!" said Jimmy. "Did you hear that?"

"I think your house is haunted!" Said Joey.

They slowly tip toed, and peeked into the bedroom to find nothing unusual.

"What's going on here?" asked Joey.

"Don't look at me" said Jimmy. A very loud crash came from the living room. They quickly ran to see what it was. Walking into the living room they noticed glass all over the floor. The front window had been smashed. Ice cold chills ran up and down Jimmy's back as he called out. "Help Dad, where are you?"

The phone rang and he was about to pick it up when he had remembered what happened earlier. "Let it ring Joey." Said Jimmy. "Don't go near that phone!

"How did the window break?" asked Joey after the phone stopped ringing.

"I don't know." Said Jimmy. "But I have an idea! Sit down in that chair and don't move one little inch."

"Where are you going Jimmy?" said Joey nervously.

"I've got something in my bedroom." He said.

"What is it? Asked Joey.

"It's a secret. I can't tell anyone. Not even you!" Jimmy said.

"But I'm your best friend." Said joey.

"Just sit still and please do not move, no matter what!" said Jimmy focefully.

He went into his bedroom leaving poor frightened Joey all alone in a room with a shattered window. Joey nervously looked about the room and thought he saw a shadow move on the floor, but it was just his imagination. The blue sky became dark grey as thick black clouds slowly rolled in. Soon the sky flashed with lightning, then the phone rang. He got up to answer it, but stopped himself when he remembered what Jimmy had told him.

Marcus Bruce

A sudden bright flash lit up the whole room, a loud crackle of
thunder made the room rattle.

"Joey!" came a raspy voice out of nowhere. "Joey, answer the
phone!" The phone began to ring again making Joey shake with
fear.

"Jimmy" shouted Joey. "Come here!" But there was only
silence. "Jimmy!" Joey shouted again half sitting in the
chair. The door knob began to move, slowly at first, but soon,
it wiggled quickly form side to side. Joey, who could take
no more, got up from the chair and ran into Jimmmy's room.
"Jimmy!" screamed Joey as he burst through the door. "I'm too
scared!" But inside Jimmy's small room, kneeling on the floor
was a giant greenish man with large golden ear rings and a
light green sheet wrapped around his enourmous head. Joey could
hardly believe his eyes. Sweat formed on his forehead, his
throat went completely dry, but he forced out a warning to his
frined. "Look out Jimmy, a monster!" He turned quicky, ran out
of the room and right smack into a man on his knees in Jimmy's
living room. "Help!" he screamed.

"Calm down Joey, what's the matter?" said the man.

"Mr. Jumpferjoy!" said Joey in amazement. "Where were you?"

"I went to the store to buy some things." He answered.

Joey looked quickly over his shoulder at Jimmy's room. "You
better help Jimmy. He's in trouble!" Said joey as he ran out
the door and down the street.

"Jimmy?" asked Mr. Jumpferjoy. "Are you all right?"

"Sure Dad, what's the matter?" said Jimmy calmly, walking
out of his room.

"Your friend Joey said you were in some type of trouble."
Answered his father.

"We were just playing."

The Amazing Adventures of Jimmy Jumpferjoy

"Well you should have been more careful. Now I'll have to
replace that window that you broke!"

"But we didn't break it Dad!" said Jimmy. "Honest."

"Well, do me a favor and clean up this mess!" said his
father. If you didn't do it, I'd like to know who did."

Mr Jumpferjoy left Jimmy, went into his bedroom and closed
the door. Jimmy went into his room and also closed the door. He
rubbed the crystal ball and called out his genie.

"I'm sorry I frightened your little friend, Master." said
the genie quietly.

"That's okay!" said Jimmy. "Will you fix the window in the
front room?" The genie out stretched his arms, and it was done.
The glass pieces flew together, looking as though nothing had
ever happened, back into the window frame.

"Now make Joey forget he ever saw you!"

"I'm sorry Master. That I can not do!"

"Why not?" asked Jimmy. "I thought you could do anything!"

"I have many strong powers, but I am afraid I can not
control people's feelings." I can not erase their memory, or
make them feel emotion like love or hate. There is a force more
powerful than I in this universe!" said the genie sadly.

"But you let me live in my dream!" Said Jimmy helplessly. "I
can't let Joey know I have a genie!"

"There's only one way I can think of, Master." Said the
genie. "You must travel to the Valley of the Deamons. There you
must take the powder from the pollen of the Moonflower. If you
are able to take it back, you'll sprinkle it over your friend's
head. He will forget all that has happened."

"But why can't I just wish for it?" asked Jimmy.

"It's protected by the scarlet fingoes. Little evergy
bugs that can take all powers right out of me. I'd be just as
helpless as you are." He answered.

"Then please tell me how to get to the Valley of the
Deamons!' said Jimmy bravely.

"Climb aboard the Magic Carpet and ask to be taken there."
Said the genie. "Your carpet knows the way!

"I'm taking my Superhero costume too!" said Jimmy.

"One other thing Master." Said the powerful genie. "I
understand that you have some type of evil force inside your
home. The moonflower pollen, when rubbed on your feet, will rid
any evil force forever!"

"Then I have no choice!" said Jimmy. "Thank you genie."
The genie vanished back into the crystal ball and Jimmy took
the rainbow colored carpet out of the closet. He sat on it
and gave the command. "Take me to the Valley of the Deamons!"
Suddenly the whole room began to dissolve. Jimmy found himself
floating high above roof tops. Strange people around him were
flying about and he notice he could see right through them.
Their eyes were opened but never moved or blinked, as they
passed right through one another. Some of them had colorful
glows about their bodies, others did not. Jimmy quickly put on
his Superhero costume and was instantly ready for any trouble.
The carpet traveled through the heavens going through trees and
even ground as though Jimmy himself were a ghost.

"I wonder what Kind of weird place this is!" he said to
himself. Looking to the far left and far right he noticed he
was surrounded by sharp rugged mountains. The carpet slipped
downward and he felt his stomach tickle. Like the feeling of
the swings at the playground. The bright colors swriling around
him were ultraviolet and infrared. The flight ended with the

carpet gliding into a bright infrared river. Strangely enough,
the carpet did not sink, but rode the water bending with every
ripple. Jimmy noticed that the red liquid moved faster and
faster until he and the carpet were pulled over a waterfall.
While falling, the carpet became airborne again. The Magic
Carpet soon landeed on the ground. This time nearest the edge
of a giant hole in the dirt. "Wonder what that could be?" said
Jimmy as he stood on the very edge looking down. Suddenly, a
big gust of wind blew Jimmy right inside of the hole. He was
falling like a lead weight into a dark endless pit. "No need
to worry!" he said calmly to himself, with his super powers he
threw his body into the dirt and rock into a dark cave. Inside
he saw a dim red glow, for the river flowing abone ground
was also beneath the surface. Two tall slimy creatures with
glowing blue eyes saw Jimmy approaching. They took out their
kisser pistols, shooting several powerful rays directly at him.
However the forcefield surrounding Jimmy's suit stopped the
laser blasts from even getting close to him. The rays bounced
off like sunshine in a mirror. As the Superhero Jimmy Jay, he
reacted fast. He took out his freeze gun, stopping the slimy,
wet earthworm-like creatures. On the floor of the cave there
was a dim yellow glowing line. Jimmy followed it. As he walked
slowly down the cavern he could see many other glowing blue
eyes peeking around large rocks and boulders. "This must be the
place!" he said to himself, rubbing his chin.

He followed the line until it ended. Being so dark he could
barely see. He lost his footing on the edge of a cliff and went
straight down into molten lava. Again, his force field did
not allow him to become hurt. More slimy cratures came out of
the walls and blasted out more bright laser fire. Jimmy flew
to the ceiling, stuck his feet there, took out his freeze gun

and froze them. He then walked upside down like an ant on the
ceiling of the cave. As he walked, he fell upward through a
trap door, into an all white room. "Where the heck am I now?"
he asked. In the white room was a tomato-red door. Jimmy opened
the red door and there was a dark room just as red. In the red
room was a blue door. Openiing the door, he found himself in a
large blue room. Believe it or not, inside the blue room was
a green door. Beyond the green door was a green room with a
yellow door. "This isn't funny anymore!" said Jimmy. He quickly
opened the yellow door only to find a very yellow room and
inside the yellow room, a red door. On the red door was a note.
Jimmy read the note. It said: 'Follow the clouds wherever they
may go, but remain yourself. If you don't you will crumble.
Search for yourself and speak the truth with a wise tongue.
Reman silent, if little things bother you, remain clever; if
big ones do, belive what you believe and keep an open mind.
Watch out for cold eyes. Don't let them freeze you.' Jimmy tore
off the door, turned it over and saw more writing on the other
side. It read: 'She came to me softly, I was her choice. She
came with a whisper, she came with a voice, a sparkling jewel,
she was there when I needed. When she warned of disaster, the
warnings I heeded. She told the truth. Never once, did she lie.
I felt a warm tingle when she was nearby. My soul would soar
freely and my soul would fly high.' Jimmy scatched his puzzled
head saying, "I wonder what this means?" He opened the red door
to a large red room. In the red room was a large blue door.
"I'm going around in circles!" said Jimmy frustrated.

    "Stop. Do not go through the blue door." Said a calm woman's
voice softly. "Instead, go back through the door you just came
in. Only then, will you be on your way to the Moonflower!"

Jimmy opened the red door and to his astonishment, he
was standing out of the never ending rooms, but now he faced
something else. A flaming wall of fire.

"Your Superhero costume will not help you here young Jimmy."
Said the calm voice. "For the fire does not burn your body, but
burns your mind! To escape, all the evil ideas that come when
walking through the fire, think no thoughts." Jimmy tightly
closed his eyes and tried to put away any thoughts he had.
When he opened his eyes, he saw odd looking people sitting in
a circle laughing right at him. They offered him things to
eat that looked delicious but he reminded himself, 'think no
thoughts no matter what, think no thoughts!' They tempted him
with things that would only make his life miserable. When he
refused, they coldly laughed at him and pointed their fingers.

"No thoughts Jimmy!" said the woman's voice. "No thoughts!"
Jimmy closed his eyes and saw darkness. He walked slowly 'till
he was out of the fire.

"I made it." He said.

"You must be very careful. "Said the voice. "There's more
danger to be sure!"

As Jimmy silently creeped through the caverns, he could hear
strange music playing. Before he knew it, he was standing in
a roomfull of people laughing and talking. A little boy with
pointed ears said. "Hello Jimmy." He picked up a cup and said,
"Drink this." "Think no thoughts!" said Jimmy. The boy vanished
into thin air. "The Cramanians work through anger and fear,
beware!" said the calm voice.

Jimmy walked through the dark cave when an arrow swiftly
flew from out of no where and struck him in the middle of his
stomach. But he did not bleed. It shocked him because it went

right through the ulitmate force field. He went to grab the
arrow, but it vanished.

"Keep walking in a straight path." said the voice. "Never
take the crooked path." Jimmy could see what she was talking
about when he almost walked on a road that looked very much
like a snake.

Suddenly a large body fell in front of him, splatterd like a
water baloon, and turned into thousands of crawling spiders.

"Do not be afraid." Said the voice. "Everything is all
right."

"Thanks," said Jimmy. I hope you never leave me. I need your
protection always!"

"I will come by from time to time, but I can not live in
your world!" said the soft voice.

Jimmy Jumpferjoy, feeling very tired from walking, rested
on a rock and began to whistle songs to himself. All of a
sudden a large wall in the cave opened up, glowing as bright
and as beautiful as ever, it was the Moonflower. Jimmy smiled
as he grabed a handful of pollen off of the flower and stuffed
it into his utility belt. "Well I got what I came for," said
Jimmy. "I thank you for your help, whoever you are!" Jimmy felt
a tingle up and down his spine, like magic fingers tickling him
from the inside of his body. Using his super powers, he flew
through the dirt and the rocks, making his way to the surface.
He called his Magic Carpet, it came to him and carried him
back to his room. He took off his superhero costume and went
directly to Joey's house.

When Joey answered the door he said, "Jimmy, how come you
didn't run, there was a gigantic green monster in your room. He
looked like a genie or something!"

"I don't know what you're talking about, you must have ben dreaming!" said Jimmy. "Well, you know as well as I do that we were not dreaming." Said Joey. "So don't lie to me!"

"Well don't say I didn't try!" answered Jimmy. He took out a handful of glowing pollen and sprinkled some over Joey's head.

"What the heck are you doing?" asked Joey, as he wiped the powdery stuff off of his hair.

"Do you remember that genie in my room?" asked Jimmy.

"What are you talking about?" asked Joey.

"Good!" said Jimmy, pleased with himself. "Now take off your shoes."

"Why?" asked Joey.

"I've got some great foot powder. It makes you feel like you float when you walk." Said Jimmy with a smile.

"Is that the junk you threw all over my head?" asked Joey.

"Please," Jimmy begged, "Just do it."

"No!" answered Joey with a frown.

"Well, watch me!" Jimmy took off his shoes and socks. He then rubbed the pollen on his left foot. Then he rubbed some on his right foot. "Boy, does this feel good!" he said happily.

"Feels good?" asked Joey.

"Sure does!" said Jimmy.

"Well let me try some." Said joey.

"Here you are my friend." said Jimmy as he poured some powder into Joey's hand.

Off went the shoes and socks. Joey rubbed some on his feet. He started to walk in a circle. When he turned to Jimmy and said, "Hey! This feels like powdered glass!"

"No more ghosts!" screamed Jimmy throwing up his arms. "This is Magic Powder!"

Marcus Bruce

"Who ever heard of magic foot powder!" said Joey disgustedly.

"Forget it!" said Jimmy, and he went back to his home feeling very tired.

END

Chapter 6

DARK GLASSES AND STRANGERS

"This has got to be one of the windiest days of the whole year!" said Jimmy to himself; for the warm summer air was flowing rapidly through the dark blue sky in a wild untamed fashion.

Jimmy had decided that he was becoming much too lazy; the genie was doing everything for him. So on this very windy day Jimmy Jumpferjoy gathered up old newspaper, wood, tape, some old rags and glue to build a home made kite. He carefully tied the wood together to make a cross, wrapping string around the middle to hold it. He then took the newspaper and taped it all together. He used his old scissors to cut the shape he wanted and used glue to hold the newspaper and wood together. When he finished building his kite, he found a ten year old can of spray paint. Carefully holding down the kite in the wild wind outside, he gave the kite a bright gold color. Jimmy was so pleased with his work that he decided the genie should give him a brand new camera. Soon the paint dried and he went out into the wind.

It was so strong that at times it seemed as if one hundred invisible hands were pushing him backwards. The golden painted newspaper fluttered quickly. The wooden sticks bent this way and that. All around him things were being carried off. Small paper cups were dragged down the street. Loose candy wrappers joined fallen leaves in a swirling twirling dance towards the clouds. Even the birds were flipping in the wind.

Jimmy was stubborn and had made up his mind. "I know in my heart you will fly higher than any other kite, because I made you by hand," he said, "and I shall name you 'Golden Kite the First'. Proud of the name and the fact that he could hear someone yell: 'It'll never make it! If the trees don't get it, the wind will tear it apart!' But he didn't care what they said.

He was going to 'Kite Hill', about to fly his home made wonder. The cool wind on 'Kite Hill' was more powerful and even stronger. Poor Jimmy knew he was in for trouble. First he ran with the kite as the wind sucked it up into the air. The weak string was pulled so tight, it snapped.

After he tied the two torn ends together, he had it in the air once more, letting out string a little at a time. He gave it enough to keep it up. Watching the kite with gleaming eyes, he said. "Boy, when you want to go, you go!" He smiled happily as the kite climbed for a cloud free blue sky.

It became smaller and smaller as it went further away; beginning to look very much like a twinkling star. 'Golden Star' whispered Jimmy to himself.

"I changed my mind. You look more like a golden star!" He tied the string to a large brownish branch on the ground and took the new camera from the camera case. "I'll take a perfect picture of a perfect kite!" He said. But looking into the camera's viewfinder, everything was much smaller. The kite looked like nothing more than a little golden sparkle. "Hey!" said jimmy, angrily to himself. "That's not fair!" The kite zigzagged back and forth in the windy sky as he pushed the camera button. "Doesn't make a difference how far you are Golden Star. I'll take a picture of you anyway. I'll blow it up afterwards if I have to!" But even as Jimmy took aim at the wiggling kite, something silverish moved back and forth inside of the camera viewer.

Marcus Bruce

"What the heck was that thing?" he asked himself jerking the viewer from his eyes.

The round silver object was much larger that Jimmy's small kite, but it looked as if the object was directly over it. He put his small camera back to his eye and began to snap pictures of the bright silverish object. Something about the movement and the way it was round and silver brought back memories of being on Mars in the past. After he took all the pictures that were on the film, he turned the camera's viewfinder backwards and he could see the object much closer. Almost like looking through a telescope.

The shiny object moved in a half circle, then went straight up at a very fast pace. Within seconds it was back at the same exact place. It rested for a brief minute, and then slowly, moved to the right. It stopped, and then moved to the left. It rested again and began to follow the movements of the kite.

Within five minutes it moved quickly out of Jimmy's sight. "I'd better pull in Golden Star!" He said, instantly to himself. Then he smiled saying, "I have a real photo of a UFO, I'll show everyone at school!" He untied the string from the branch after he had put away the camera and gently pulled the kite to the ground. Soon he was running as fast as his nervous legs could carry him. He dashed by the kids on the swings.

"Hey kid, we saw your kite, it's beautiful!" someone said. But Jimmy wasn't thinking about his kite. He wanted to hurry home and develop the film.

While running, he lost the grip on his kite and as he turned the corner, the wind quickly whisked the kite from out of his hands and dragged it down the street. The wind lifted the kite off of the ground, spun it around, and tossed it into the near-by trees. Being worried and not thinking clearly, Jimmy grabbed the string. He yanked it too hard. The wood snapped in half, and Golden Star became a useless pile of gold-painted newspaper tangled in wood splinters.

"Oh well," said Jimmy, to himself, as he viewed the mess scooting along the ground. "At least I have a picture of a real live UFO." He held his camera tight and hurried home to see the photo.

Entering his room, he felt his heart beating faster and excitement fogged his head. "Come out genie and make it snappy!" he said as he rubbed the crystal ball. As usual the room was filled with green smoke and the powerfully large genie appeared on his knees to his little master.

"What is it that you want, oh mighty master?" he asked in a powerful voice. No one was home so Jimmy didn't care how loud he talked.

"Develop these pictures!" he said as he handed a roll of film to his greenish genie.

"They have stores for that," said the genie.

"Can't wait," Jimmy insisted anxiously, "I've got to see them now!"

With that, the genie blew steam on the roll of film and instantly it was transformed into pictures.

"These are too small," said Jimmy. "Could you blow them up?

"Make them bigger?" asked the genie.

"Yeah!" said jimmy quickly. The genie blinked his eyes and the pictures were much larger. Jimmy had large poster sized pictures of both Golden Star and the Unknown object.

"Thank you genie," said Jimmy pleasantly.

"You're welcome," answered the genie. "Is that all you want?"

Marcus Bruce

"Yeah!" said Jimmy, "that's all." The genie rolled his large eyes and vanished back into the crystal ball.

Time passed and night came quickly. 'I'd better send this to the Air Force,' Jimmy thought to himself, 'to see if it's the real thing and not some kind of joke!" He went to another room, picked up the phone and dialed. "Information, can I have the number to Jackson's Air Force base?" he asked and a woman on the phone told him what number to dial.

After dialing, there came a very low voice which sounded very important.

"May I help you?" said the man's voice.

"Yes," said Jimmy. "I have a picture of an unknown object."

"You mean a UFO?" asked the man.

"That's right!" said Jimmy.

"I'm sorry, we can't help you," said the man. "The Air Force no longer collects UFO information. Try a UFO research group, maybe they can help you."

"All right," said Jimmy. "bye."

Jimmy went into his bedroom to look carefully at the pictures before making another phone call. There came a loud knock at the door in the front room.

"I'll get it." said Mr. Jumpferjoy. When he answered the door, there were two men wearing very dark sun glasses. Both of them had a funny odor about them, like the smell of a hard boiled egg.

"May we speak to your son?" asked one of the men standing a little taller than Mr. Jumpferjoy.

"Why?" asked Mr. Jumpferjoy. "What did he do?"

"We are special agents," said the other man calmly, "we just want to ask him a few questions."

"Who's there James?" asked Mrs. Jumpferjoy.

"Special agents," answered Jimmy's father.

"Oh my!" said Mrs. Jumpferjoy, somewhat surprised. "What has my little boy done?"

"He's done nothing wrong ma'am," answered the first agent. "We would like to ask just a few short questions."

"Why are you here then?" asked Mr. Jumferjoy.

"Top Secret." said the second agent.

"That's right." said the first agent. "Now, can we see your son?"

"Well all right," answered Mrs. Jumpferjoy. "I hope everything is OK!"

They led the strange visitors up to Jimmy's door and gave a couple of light knocks.

"Come in," said Jimmy.

"Please wait out here," said the second agent as they entered Jimmy's room.

"Good evening Jimmy," he said smiling. "How are you?"

"Who are you?" asked Jimmy.

"I'm a friend." answered the man with dark glasses.

"I don't know you!" said Jimmy. "Get out of my room, or I'll tell my Mom and Dad!"

"Your parents let us in!" said the man softly.

"Well, what do you want with me!" asked Jimmy, getting angry by the minute.

"We just want the pictures!" he said.

"What pictures?" asked Jimmy.

"The pictures you took today," said the agent forcefully, "hand them over!"

"How did you know about the pictures? I didn't even send them out to be developed." Said Jimmy more confused than ever.

Marcus Bruce

"It's important to us that you do not show those photographs to anyone!" said the agent.

"Why not?" asked Jimmy. "They're my pictures."

"Just hand them over!" said the stranger.

Jimmy didn't know anything about the stranger so he tried to trick him. "I don't know why anyone would want to take away photos of a little boy's kite.

"We know about the pictures," said the agent. "You can't fool us!"

"But those are my pictures and I want them. I want to show all of my friends," said Jimmy sadly.

"If you don't hand them over," said the agent sternly, "you may never see your parents again!"

Jimmy Laughed. "Ha! You can't harm my parents!"

The agent stepped closer to Jimmy and whispered, "We know about the crystal ball too." Poor Jimmy became very frightened, his knees locked, his mouth dried out and his stomach began to hurt. Nobody, but nobody could know about the genie. These people were not really agents, at least not from this planet. He suddenly felt he had better hand over the pictures or let the whole world know his secret.

"Um, you know about the crystal ball?" he asked as he nervously cleared his throat.

"The pictures!" said the man dressed in black as he held out his hand. Jimmy was slow to get the pictures, and even slower to hand them over. He took one final look at the picture of the UFO above 'Golden Star', his kite, and with eyes watering, watched the man leave his room. "I'd better keep an eye on them," said Jimmy to himself as he opened his bedroom door. He saw the man thank his parents and walk out with the pictures tucked under his arms. The other one carefully closed the

The Amazing Adventures of Jimmy Jumpferjoy

door behind himself. As they drove off, Jimmy went quickly back into his bedroom, picked up his Telescope of Wonder and looked inside only to see a long black car driving off with a strange purple gas coming from beneath. Without any warning, the car slowly vaporized. Jimmy put the telescope away slightly stunned. His father entered the room; his mother leaned on the doorway. Mr. Jumpferjoy tapped his son on the shoulder.

"Jimmy, one of the men explained to us that you witnessed an accident. He told up that your information could help save some important lives."

"They lied!" said Jimmy. He looked at his mother and father. "It's top secret. They told me I couldn't tell you!"

Later that night his mother tucked him in and his father told him not to worry. Jimmy fell asleep and met Jilly Applejelly in her world.

"Jimmy, how come you look so sad?" she asked as she walked toward him from behind a dark purple tree.

"I don't know Jilly. I built a kite and flew it up in the air, then a UFO came by. I took pictures of the kite and the UFO. The next thing I knew, some guys came in and took away my pictures!"

"Well, who were they?" she asked him.

"They claimed to be special agents, but Jilly, they knew about the crystal ball!"

"Oh no!" said Jilly covering her mouth with her hand. "How did they ever know?"

"I can't figure it out, but all they wanted were my pictures!"

Jilly patted Jimmy on his back and said, "Don't worry Jimmy. I'll help you as much as I can. I promise!"

Marcus Bruce

"How can you help?" he asked "You don't know who they are, do you?"

"No," she answered. "But in case they say they'll take your crystal ball or say that they'll hurt your parents, my genie can help!" She sat down on the ground and invited Jimmy to do the same.

"They told me I might never see my parents, but that was if I didn't give them the pictures!" said jimmy. "We'll, just in case." said Jilly quickly, "we'd better do something fast." She rubbed her red ring and called out her genie.

"Yes, oh mistress Jilly?" asked the genie as she appeared out of the pink smoke.

"Please protect Jimmy's crystal ball and his family!"

"OK," said the genie. "First, I will put an invisible force field around the crystal ball so that only Jimmy will be able to touch it."

"Will this work against non-humans too?" he asked.

"Yes," said the genie.

"How long will it last?" asked Jimmy.

"For about three months." said the genie.

"Secondly, I will place a silver coated shield invisible to the human eye about your parents so nothing can happen to them, also around the things most important to you, like the house and car."

The genie spread forth her mighty arms and her body glowed a bright yellow. She clapped her hands and sparks of magic flew outward. "It's done." She said and in a sparkle she was gone.

"Now I bet you want your pictures back, right Jimmy?" asked Jilly.

"Right," he said.

"Well, what should we do first?" she asked.

The Amazing Adventures of Jimmy Jumpferjoy

"Wait, before we try to figure this whole thing out. Let me tell you something," said Jimmy.

"What?" asked Jilly.

"Well, before I found the crystal ball, I used to be very, very lonely. I didn't go anywhere or do anything special. And I didn't really have any friends I could trust. I used to be pretty bored most of the time. Wherever I was, I used to try counting the lines on the sidewalk or balance on the edge of a street curb. But now, I'm never bored. I'm so busy that I don't have time to get bored. Most of all, I've discovered my greatest friend and she was just a dream away."

"Jilly, when you say you'll help me. I trust you. I trust you even more than Joey."

"Well, why shouldn't you trust me?" asked Jilly. "Here in my land, no one ever lies, or tricks you and everyone is helpful. Not just me."

"But you are special," said Jimmy. "You're smarter than anybody I know too."

"Everyone is smart in their own way," she answered. "When people in my land want to gain more information they meet with the wonderful wise wizards."

"Who are these wise wizards?" Jimmy asked.

"They are like teachers. They will answer any question you have."

"Maybe they can help me!" said Jimmy, raising one fist in the air.

Jilly lead the way to a beautiful place where there were many deep steps leading toward the underground. At the bottom of the stairs was a large wooden door. With a knocker that looked like a large human skull. When Jilly touched the knocker, a loud horn blew. Slowly the door opened. Inside was

a blinding light. Three figures wearing cone shaped hats were
sitting in front of a small screen. One stood and spoke while
the others remained sitting with their eyes closed.

"Question?" he asked, and gave a wink to Jilly.

"Um, yes," said Jimmy. "I want to know who the special
agents were that came to my house." The wizard placed his hands
on Jimmy's forehead and on the screen appeared everything that
had happened with the special agents. When the screen went
blank, the wizard spoke.

"These people that came to your house are not from your
world. They are agents of another kind. They are known in other
worlds as Cramanians. That is your answer, good day." The
wizards walked out of the palace, and on to a field of bright
red grass.

"Cramanians!" said Jimmy suddenly. "This could be more
trouble than we can take care of ourselves. We'll need more
people."

"What are you planning to do?" asked Jilly.

"In the morning, I'm going out and find those kids that were
on the swings. Then we'll form a spy club and search for the
agents," he answered.

Slowly waking up, Jimmy wiped his tired eyes. Orange,
early morning sunlight filled his room. He washed up and ate
breakfast. Being sleepy, he yawned as he sat at the breakfast
table until nine-thirty. Then Jimmy went back into his room.
There he took out the crystal ball and quietly called his
genie. When the genie came, Jimmy wanted Jilly Applejelly in
his world. The genie granted the wish and Jilly stepped out of
her world and into his.

Jimmy smiled and said, "Jilly, will you join my spy club?"

"I'd be glad to!" said Jilly and off they went in search
of the kids that were on the swings. They arrived at the park
and found no one there; so Jimmy passed the time showing Jilly
how to use the swings and slide. She laughed, giggled, and had
great fun.

Lunch time soon came and went. At twelve-thirty four,
children walked directly to the swings.

"Hey, were any of you guys here yesterday?" asked Jimmy.

"Yeah, we were here." answered a little girl. "You're the
kid with the golden kite, right?"

"That's right," said Jimmy, "and this is my friend Jilly."

After they had learned each other's names, Jimmy asked
them if they had seen anything strange or unusual. All of them
agreed that they had seen a flying saucer.

"Did anyone have a camera?" Jimmy asked curiously.

"I think Mark did," said a little boy named Tommy.

"Which one of you is Mark?" asked Jimmy.

"He's at home." said Tommy.

"Let's go see him."

They soon left the park and walked a few blocks to Mark's
house. When they rang the door bell, no one answered. But the
curtains opened slowly as if someone were peeking out.

"Hey Mark, it's me!" shouted Tommy. Mark closed the curtains
and slowly opened the front door. He carefully explained to
them his unusual experience, as Tommy, Ricky, Sammy, Suzy,
Jimmy and Jilly listened. They began to feel cool chills in
their bodies.

"They said if I showed anyone the pictures, my pet bird
would never be seen forever," Mark said, as he finished his
last sentence.

Marcus Bruce

"And they were wearing dark sunglasses at night?" asked Jimmy.

"Yeah," said Mark. "I watched them drive off and you won't believe me, but the whole car vanished before my eyes!"

"They came to my house too!" said Jimmy. "I saw that car disappear! What we should do, is form a secret agent club and search for those strange men."

"What if we find them?" asked Suzy.

"Report all information to me!" said Jimmy. "We will meet at the park until we can get some kind of club house."

"At the swings?" asked Ricky.

"Right," said Jimmy, "the first thing we will all need is a code book."

"Why don't you make some up, Jimmy, and we'll see you at the park tomorrow at twelve-thirty," said Mark eagerly."

"We'll need a special hand shake," said Ricky, "like in the movies."

"How about if we grab thumbs to shake?" asked Tommy.

They all agreed and after trading phone numbers, they all left for home.

In his room, which was cluttered from looking for pens and paper, Jimmy Jumpferjoy was fast at work on the code books. "Let me see," said Jimmy with blue pen in hand. "For UFO we'll use the word 'plate'. For men with dark sunglasses we'll call them the 'creeps'. Before long he had written something that looked like this:

UFO	=	Plate
Men with dark sunglasses	=	The Creeps
Pictures	=	Paint
Secret	=	Quiet
Spy	=	Sheek

Friends	=	Company
Agents	=	Bonds
Special	=	One
Threat	=	Calm
Hide	=	Open
Run	=	Walk

Also, he wrote down a coded name for each person in the group; Tommy became, Slick, Ricky was renamed Space, Sammy was now called Time, Suzy was named Venus, Jilly was now Rainbow, and Mark's code name was Snap. Jimmy named himself Gold, and everything was set. He had his genie make copies of the code words inside little booklets for his new friends. Jimmy made sure he had everyone's code name in each code booklet. He had Jilly join him and at twelve-thirty, they all met each other in the park at the swings.

"OK," said Jimmy, "since its so hot today, why don't we sit under the trees?"

"Good idea!" said Suzy. "My throat's all dry anyway. Once under the trees, Jimmy passed out the code books and everyone was very pleased.

"Do you like your new names?" Jimmy asked, "'cause if you don't, we could change them."

"I like my code name!" said Tommy.

Everyone claimed that their code name fit, so Jimmy said, "OK, let's have roll call." After everyone was called, and of course everyone was there, Jimmy asked, "Are there any questions?"

"Yes," said Ricky.

"Space," said Jimmy, using the code name. "What is your question?"

"Will we have to pay dues?"

"No dues!" said Jimmy.

Another hand went up. "Snap," said Jimmy.

"What if we can't make a meeting?" asked Mark.

"Call me at home and I'll give you coded information," said Jimmy "any more questions?" No one had any. "OK, I want us to spread out and ask friends, neighbors and people on the street if they have seen anything unusual in the sky. Ask them if they took a picture and if the creeps came to their house." He put his hand on his chin and then said. "OK, listen up. These are the groups; Space, and slick, Venus Snap and Time, Me and Rainbow. We meet same place, same time tomorrow. Let's go!" They took different streets and soon began to ask people questions.

Standing in the doorway of a drugstore was a skinny man smoking a long cigar. Jimmy Jumpferjoy walked up to him and began to ask questions. "Excuse me sir, are you from around here?"

"No," said the man quietly.

"Were you around here two days ago at around noon time?"

"Yes." answered the man.

"Did you happen to see anything unusual?"

"Yes I did." answered the man. "You mean a silverish object that zigzagged in the sky?"

"Well I was wondering . . ." Jimmy started to say.

"First I saw this golden kite in the sky. Then, from out of no where I saw this thing that was bigger than an airplane," said the man.

"Well, I was wondering . . ." said Jimmy again.

"Then it zoomed off. Strangest thing I every saw in my life." said the man.

"Well I was wondering if you took any pictures?" asked
Jimmy.

"You bet I did!" answered the man. "But some Air Force guys
came and took my pictures away. I tell you, one just doesn't
have the privacy any more."

"What did they look like?" asked Jimmy.

"Well," said the man, "they were both about the same size
and they looked more like spies than Air Force. Some strange
thing too; they smelt like hard boiled eggs."

"Anything else?" asked Jimmy, hoping that the guy had
something more to add.

"Well, they came to my home at night. I was wondering why
they both were wearing sunglasses. By the way kid, why do you
want to know all this?"

"Because those men took away my pictures too!" said Jimmy,
"that's why."

"Thank you very much," said Jilly, "come on Jimmy."

"Thanks," said Jimmy, and they went straight to Jimmy's
house.

As they walked down the street they passed two strangers,
one said to the other, "Is that the one?" Jimmy and Jilly
looked at each other and walked faster.

"Mom," said Jimmy bursting through the door, "this is my
friend Jilly Applejelly."

"Nice to meet you Jilly," said Mrs. Jumpferjoy. "Jimmy, you
received a couple of phone calls by some children with weird
names. Names like Slick, Space and others. Do you know who I'm
talking about?"

"They're in my club mom," said Jimmy. He made his phone
calls and learned that there were at least four other people
that had seen the object, but only one had a camera. Two men

had come by saying they were with the FBI and took away the film.

Jimmy turned to Jilly and said with a smile, "I think we're on to something big."

The next day at the park, Slick, Space, Time and Venus and Snap all showed up at the swings.

"Well," said Jimmy, "the creeps have been all around this town! They've been taking the paint from people everywhere. Seems like when people take paint of the plate, the creeps show up. I just hope those quiet bonds don't sheek on us."

"Gold," said Mark, "where do we open if they try to calm us?"

"I'm afraid," said Jimmy, "there's no place to walk. However, we should try to protect each other because we are company. I do have a quiet weapon I could use if they try to attack.

"OK group, keep your eyes open and watch out for strangers in the neighborhood. They just might try to move in! Swings, same time," said Jimmy. And they all went off to their homes.

The next day, Snap didn't show up for the meeting. He didn't show up the day after that either. Something was wrong and Jimmy knew it. He called Snap up and was told that the creeps had the phone bugged. Snap said he would call later if he could. But Jimmy couldn't wait. He took Jilly with him to Snap's home. When he knocked on the door, Snap silently peeked out of the curtains. When he saw that it was Jimmy and Jilly, he opened the door and whispered, "Be very quiet, now follow me." He led them over to the curtains and opened them slightly. "See that blue car?" he whispered.

"Yeah," said Jilly quietly.

"He's been here for three days and I've never seen the guy get out of it. A note came in the mail and it said, 'give it up or your bird will disappear.' That note came the same day we formed our spy group. Well, now my bird is gone and I got another note saying my dog will be next. I tried but I'm sorry. I can't be a spy any more. I hope you'll understand."

"OK," said Jimmy, "Jilly, maybe we should go." Snap opened the door and that was the last they saw of him. Jimmy had the genie give him a tape recorder to use in interviews after that, in case people were forced to change their stories.

The next day he found the stranger at the drug store. He asked the man to repeat his story, but the man claimed he never saw a UFO, or the two Air Force men. One by one all his friends dropped out until it was only he and Jilly.

"Well Jilly, what do we do now? We've lost all our help!"

"I hope nothing happens to them!" said Jilly, "they are all so nice."

"Jilly," said Jimmy thinking quickly. "Have your genie give them invisible silver shields to!"

"OK Jimmy," said Jilly Applejelly. She rubbed her red ring. The genie appeared through the pink clouds of smoke, Jilly asked for her friends to be protected. Once the wish was granted, Jimmy decided to locate the Elements.

"But why locate the Elements?" asked Jilly.

"Because if the Cramamians are here, the Elements can't be too far behind," answered Jimmy. He took his Telescope of Wonder and saw an alien base with plenty of aliens working hard. "Jilly, I believe the Elements have a base right here on Earth!"

"Really?" she asked. He nodded his head and put his telescope away.

Marcus Bruce

"Oh, I see you brought a friend over again!" said Mrs. Jumpferjoy approaching. She smiled at Jilly. "Jimmy, here is a letter for you." She handed Jimmy the letter and left. He opened the envelope but the paper inside was totally blank. He checked both sides, front and back but couldn't find a trace of writing.

"That's odd, I wonder what this is all about?" he said.

Jilly shrugged her shoulders.

"Invisible ink?" he asked.

"Why not?" said Jilly.

"Let's see," said Jimmy, and he brought Jilly to the kitchen, "first, I heat up the iron, and then I put the paper down." His mother just happened to be listening. She walked calmly into the kitchen.

"Jimmy, I'm afraid you are not allowed to play with the iron!"

"But Mom, it's very important!" he said.

"Nothing could be that important," she said sternly.

"It's for those special agents, invisible ink!" he said sadly.

"I don't ever want you to play in the kitchen," she said. "I'll let you show me what you mean this time!"

Jimmy took the iron which was set on low and ran it over the paper back and forth until the words became visible.

"It says give," said Jilly, when she saw the first word.

"Give it!" said Jimmy, when the second word became known.

"Give it up!" said his mother. "It says give it up. What does that mean?"

"I'm afraid to ask," said Jimmy.

"Jilly, I think you should leave now. I would like to speak to my son."

- 134 -

Jimmy knew Jilly couldn't leave until she went back into her world, so he said, "I'll walk Jilly home after we talk, OK Mom?"

"Well . . . OK, but Jilly, why don't you take a seat in the front room?" said Mrs Jumpferjoy.

"All right," said Jilly, as she walked out of the kitchen.

"Young man, do you care to tell me what's going on?" said Jimmy's mother.

"Those guys weren't special agents. They were lying. Now I'm afraid they might try to get me!"

"What exactly are you talking about?" asked his mother "those men were with the government, they showed us proof."

"They did?" asked Jimmy.

"Yes, and now what were you saying?" she asked.

"Oh, um . . . I was just joking!" he answered nervously.

"No more jokes like that, do you understand Jimmy!"

"Yes Mom," he answered.

Thinking quickly, he left his mother in the kitchen and said "I'll get my sweater and walk Jilly home."

"You do that!" answered his mother.

He went into his room and asked the genie to send Jilly back to her world. He put on a sweater then pretended to leave with Jilly while his mother was still in the kitchen.

"We're going," said Jimmy.

"Good-bye," said his mother. "Hurry back Jimmy, I'll have supper ready."

Jimmy Jumpferjoy walked around the block and as he approached his house he noticed the same blue car that was in front of Snap's (Mark's) house. He also noticed that there was someone inside the car.

Marcus Bruce

He crossed the street and walked slowly up along side the
car and looked in. What he saw almost made his heart stop
beating. Inside the car was a dark human-like figure with very
large eyes that glowed yellow in the dark.

"Yipes!" screamed Jimmy loudly as he turned and ran without
looking back.

"Help!" he screamed. He could feel fear in every inch of
his trembling body. "Help me, help me!!!" his feet moved faster
than he had expected, and he tripped over a rock. He didn't
have time to worry about anything; he scrambled back up and ran
to his house. He slammed and locked the door behind him.

"Don't slam that door!" yelled Mr. Jumpferjoy, who had
arrived home just minutes before.

"S-S-Sorry D-Dad!" said Jimmy, his lips quivering with
fright. He quickly walked into his room and closed the door.
He moved his dresser over and put it in front of the door.
Then he grabbed the Telescope of Wonder from under his pillow.
"Show-show me where the Elements are!" The telescope first
showed the coast of Florida, then the ocean, and at the last,
beneath the ocean, alien people working very hard.

He took out the crystal ball and rubbed it. When his genie
came out, he told the genie he wanted to go through the walls
of his room with his carpet. He then asked the genie to bring
back Jilly Applejelly.

With a pocket full of magic berries and the Telescope
of Wonder in his hand, Jimmy snapped his fingers and said,
"Go carpet!" Jimmy and Jilly and the carpet went up right
through the ceiling. They flew for some time before they saw
the Florida coast. He gave a berry to Jilly and took one for
himself; for the berries allowed them to breathe underwater.
Down into the sea they went with a big splash. Jilly rubbed her

ring and had her genie dig a deep hole down beneath the ocean floor. The genie returned to the ring and before long Jimmy and Jilly were standing inside a great hallway.

They walked, but did not know just where they were going. Both heard a sharp buzzing noise and from around the corner came a bright red beam of light moving slowly towards them.

"Run Jilly, run!" said Jimmy, in a fit of excitement. But when they turned and ran, it was as if they were moving very slowly. The ray hit them very hard and their memory was lost.

When Jimmy opened his eyes, he saw Jilly inside a long clear tube. Looking around he saw that there were many other people sleeping in tubes. Checking his hands, he realized that his carpet and telescope were missing.

Jilly woke up and waved to Jimmy. He waved back. Then he tried yelling to her, but she couldn't hear him. He pointed to his lips and said: "Read my lips!"

Jilly nodded and pointed to her lips. "Me too!"

"Look around," said Jimmy, pointing his finger around in every direction. She looked around wrapped her arms around her body and moved her lips wide.

"I'm scared!" her lips said.

"Don't be afraid!" said Jimmy, moving his lips up and down so Jilly could understand.

Suddenly, suction entered the tube and Jilly was sucked upward quickly and out of sight.

"Wow," said Jimmy to himself, "now I'm here alone!"

"There's nothing to worry about Jimmy," said a soft voice of a woman. Jimmy looked around and saw no one. "Everything will be all right."

Marcus Bruce

"But everything is not all right!" he said anxiously,
"Jilly's gone, I'm stuck in this tube, and I don't even know if
these people are friendly.

"Don't worry, try to relax. These people are your true
friends. Please believe me. Have I ever lied to you?"

"Well, you didn't lie to me the last time you came to me,"
he said. "So I guess I can trust you." The air in the tube
moved upward pulling Jimmy up with it. After a short journey,
through the tube, he ended up standing before a group of people
that looked grey. They had very large eyes that seemed to go to
the sides of their heads. The people reminded him of Kanue. It
was then that he lost most of his fear.

Walking here and there around them were humanoids that
looked like everyday people, except that their eyes were
larger.

"Why are you here?" asked the alien in front of him.

"Cramanians are after us!" said Jimmy. The grayish alien
blinked his large eyes and a loud alarm sounded. Everyone
around became invisible. What once looked like a gigantic
bustling airplane hanger, became a very large empty cave. Only
Jimmy and the alien remained visible.

"Where are they?" asked the grey person.

"No, they didn't follow us here; they came to my house in
Artsville. The grayish alien blinked his enormous eyes once
more and everything reappeared.

"You know about the Cramanians?" asked the alien.

"Yes," said Jimmy, "Kanue told me about them!"

"You know Kanue?" asked the alien.

"Yes," said Jimmy happily, "where is he?"

"Well," answered the alien, "he's either beneath the crust of Mars, or in the Martian fourth dimension; or perhaps he's joined the many that walk on the surface of your planet.

"You mean your people are up there?" asked Jimmy looking upward.

"Yes, but no more talk!" said the alien, "business first!"

"What about Jilly Applejelly?" asked Jimmy, hoping nothing had happened to her.

"Your friend will be here in a minute. We ran tests and found her not of this world!" said the alien. She's from the seventh dimension." Two alien women brought Jilly into the room. They had very large eyes, the same grey skin, white hair, and looked very much like human women, only better.

"Jimmy, we don't have to fear these people, they are like my own," said Jilly.

"My name is Dimitri," said the alien, "you are Jimmy jumpferjoy and this is Jilly Applejelly". They both nodded.

"Have you ever traveled into the earth's future?" asked Dimitri. Both shook their heads no. "To combat the Cramanians, we must create a problem and they will have to fix it before they can cause more trouble.

Dimitri led them to the time transport machine. As they walked right into the future, they were transported to Los Angeles, California, several years into the future on a vacant lot.

"Most of California was destroyed by a gigantic earthquake, part of it broke off and became an island," said Dimitri. "On my wrist, I carry a vision scanner. You will look at it and get familiar with the current events," he said.

He held out his arm and showed Jilly and Jimmy the vision
scanner. Dimitri took a small pink glowing pill with his free
hand and was transformed into a human-looking man.

The scanner showed many things to be different, yet
strangely enough, the same. It showed dances to be different,
music had changed, cars were still around, but all had radar
and instead of gasoline, they ran on liquid hydrogen. Fruit
and vegetables were different in shape. For instance; a banana
was two feet long and looked more like a yellow watermelon.
Candy bars were smaller and the cheap ones were one hundred
dollars. Animals were changed by the scientists to look bigger
and fatter. Criminals were not put in jail, but were hypnotized
or brainwashed. If it didn't work, they were injected with
an honesty drug that turned them good. Roller coasters went
backwards, black soda pop to drink, and many other things were
here in the future.

"We must meet the proper people, and then travel to the
South Pole," said Dimitri.

He led them out of the vacant lot, and into the busy
futuristic city. They arrived at some very tall apartments and
Dimitri rang the doorbell.

"Who is it?" came a pleasant sounding woman's voice.

"Dimitri."

"Ver no dandara Sime hanso?" she asked.

"MY de kanzno met sue!" answered Dimitri."

"sunly mansoon," said the woman.

"She wanted to know who you two were," whispered Dimitri.
They looked at each other and nodded their heads. The door
opened and standing before them was an actress Jimmy had seen
when he was very young, but she had not changed one bit in the
future.

The Amazing Adventures of Jimmy Jumpferjoy

"You should be an old woman by now," said Jimmy.

The beautiful actress laughed, threw her hair back and said, "If only I were human! There are many of us on your world, from the ancient past, to the future and beyond."

"Wow," said Jimmy.

"We need information on the exact location of the Cramanians," said Dimitri.

The woman handed Dimitri a small map and kissed him on the cheek. "Good luck!" she said. They left the apartment and walked a few blocks down the street to a man that looked like a homeless bum. Dimitri snapped his fingers.

"What do you want?" asked the bum, with a bottle of wine in his hands.

"Dimitri, Cramanians!" said Dimitri,

"It's been taken care of, you have a clear passageway!" said the bum. He winked and spoke again. "Dim say dat dat zow."

"Dim say dat dat zow osee!" said Dimitri. "OK Jilly and Jimmy, we'll go back to that vacant lot, we will be picked up and we will be on our way to the Cramanian's base."

They left the big city and walked back to the vacant lot. Within seconds a large UFO with many different colored lights flew in and landed. Jimmy, Jilly and Dimitri entered the ship and like a sudden flash it zoomed toward the South Pole. "Here's the plan," said Dimitri. "We let you lose on the base. You will be protected by and energy field so when they fire their rays, nothing will affect you. I'll receive help by some of our inside men and locate their power source. From there, I will place tiny energy insects to eat their energy source. They will have to shut down their base for a long time."

"OK, we are almost there, remember, if you think you are in any trouble, close your eyes and say "Minso dragness! You will

find yourself back at the ship. Here we go." The ship crashed
through the hard ice in the South Polar Sea and traveled
through the ice cold ocean floor. Jilly and Jimmy were quickly
beamed out of the ship and put into place. Alarms rang out and
the guards shot off their bright ray guns at the two. Like
frightened rabbits Jimmy and Jilly ran as fast as they could.
They were captured by two tall ugly guards and couldn't escape.

"Minso dragness!" screamed Jilly closing her eyes tight.
Jimmy repeated the words and did the same. Both of their bodies
became white hot and the en energy force burned the hands of
the Cramanian guards. As they disappeared from the base, they
reappeared on the ship.

"Good, you're back!" said Dimitri. "Let's go!"

"Wait, what about our mission?" said Jimmy.

"It's been done!" answered Dimitri.

"Already?" asked Jilly.

"That's right!" said Dimitri.

They left the future and went back to the coast of Florida.
Jimmy said good-bye to the aliens there. Dimitri turned back
to his original form and Jilly was happy the danger was now
over. Dimti told Jimmy that he wouldn't have to use the carpet
because he would fly him back. Jimmy wrapped up his carpet,
held the Telescope of Wonder in his hands, and in two seconds
he was back home again. Jilly went back to her world and
something told Jimmy to check the mailbox. There inside, was
another letter for him. It read: `We will get you later!"

`Ha, that's what you think!' said Jimmy to himself as he
prepared for a peaceful rest in bed.

Chapter 7

VOYAGE TO A LOST ISLAND

In Jilly Applejelly's wonderful world, the weather never changes. It's almost always pleasant. That is why she and her friend Fluidica took Jimmy Jumpferjoy on a nice walk in the open countryside; without fear of rain. Jilly's eyes glistened as she began to marvel at the sights and just being there.

"Jimmy, have you ever wondered why the sky is green, the grass is red, and the air always smells so sweet?"

"No, I'm afraid not Jilly," he answered with a smile.

"Why not?" asked fluidica.

"Because, where I come from, the sky is blue, the grass is green, and the air always smells like air!"

"Oh, Jimmy!" said Jilly laughing with Fluidica, "You know what I mean!"

"Jilly, didn't you say you went to Jimmy's house?" asked Fluidica.

"Yes," said Jilly, "I went to his house first, then I went to a place called a park."

"Did you like it there?" asked Fluidica curiously.

"Well," answered Jilly, looking at Jimmy. "It's a very nice place to visit, but believe me, there's no place like home!"

"Oh, come on!" said Jimmy. He took his first finger and poked Jilly in her side until she giggled. "By the way," said Jimmy, "where are we going?"

"No where special," said Fluidica.

"Oh, that's why it feels like we've been walking around in circles," said Jimmy.

"We were! No kidding," said Jilly. "Why don't we sit down and rest for a little while."

"Good idea," said Fluidica.

"Then what'll we do?" asked Jimmy.

"Tell stories!" said Jilly.

"You first," Fluidica said.

"OK," said Jilly. "there once was a little boy named Jimmy Jumpferjoy."

"And," said Jimmy, "he met a little girl named Jilly Applejelly."

"And they all lived happily ever after!" laughed Fluidica.

The three rolled with laughter until they finally decided to play a game called true or false. Here's how the rules went; one person would tell a story. The others had to guess whether it was true, false, or half and half. Fluidica guessed correct three times in a row. Jimmy won only once and Jilly was the one to win the game.

"Can you say toy boat six times fast?" asked Jimmy. Jilly tried but became tongue tied. Fluidica did even worse.

"You do it Jimmy!" said Jilly.

"Toy boat, toy boat, toit bowl, toy boit, oh, forget it!" said Jimmy, and he laughed heartily.

"Who can say toy boit sixt times fast?" asked Fluidica excitedly.

"You do it!" said Jimmy.

"No, you!" said Fluidica.

"Why doesn't Jimmy say toy boat, boy toit ten times fast because he's so smart," said Jilly teasingly.

"Hey, wait a minute," said Jimmy, holding his hands open. "I'm not so smart. It's just that you two are so dumb!"

Marcus Bruce

"Just say it and be quiet smarty pants!" said Fluidica. However, no matter how hard he tried, Jimmy could not do it. Neither could the two girls; but they had a fun time trying. Soon everything became blurry. Jimmy knew he was waking up.

"Well, I've got to go now," he said, and everything went black.

"Breakfast!" yelled Jimmy's mother.

"Hold on!" he answered in a tired crackling voice. He put his arms behind his head and stared at the ceiling for a while. Then he climbed out of bed.

"OK, here I come," he said. He washed up and sat at the breakfast table expecting a good hot meal. "Oh no, corn flakes again!" he complained.

"You didn't mind them last week, or the week before," said his mother.

"What's the matter? Are you getting spoiled or something?"

"I'm just tired of eating the same old food all the time," he whined.

"I'm sorry son, that's all we have. We're not rich you know," she said.

"I know mom," said Jimmy, "I just wish some day we'll have many different kinds of food in the house."

"Well, you'd better keep wishing!" said his mother breathing very hard as she left the kitchen and went into her bedroom.

"Cornflakes for breakfast again, yuck!" he whispered to himself. "All I have to do is call out my genie and I could have bacon, eggs, pancakes, sausages or anything. I could have a large glass of orange juice, with toast and butter too. And if I were really hungry, I could eat . . ." he suddenly stopped talking to himself when he heard strange sounding noises coming from his mother's room. "What's that?" he said to himself.

He silently tip-toed up to his mother's door. There he saw his sad, sad, mother laying on the bed with a pillow over her face. She was crying her heart out. Jimmy suddenly felt very sorry for being so selfish and went to comfort his unhappy mother.

"I'm sorry Mom!" said Jimmy with misty eyes, "I didn't mean to make you cry!"

"You try so hard and get no where!" cried his mother with plump tear drops streaming down her very sad face. "For over four years, it seems, we haven't been able to have even one day of good luck." Her voice began to tremble. "I really wish I could offer you more Jimmy, but we just don't have any money," she said as she cried louder into the pillow.

Jimmy's own eyes began to water, as he patted her gently on the back. "Don't worry Mom, I promise we will have good luck when the time is right!" Mrs. Jumpferjoy tightly hugged her son, wiped her eyes and kissed him on the cheek.

"I keep saying the same thing Jimmy. Maybe, just maybe, it will come true."

"Mom," said Jimmy, as he wiped his own eyes, "they say dreams come true when you want them to."

His mother laughed cheerfully as the tears flowed over her cheeks and said "I really hope so."

Later that afternoon, Jimmy watched his small black and white television set. In between his programs, he saw the toy car of his dreams called 'Fire Speed Demon," the fastest toy car on wheels. "That's the one I want!" He went into his bedroom and took out his crystal ball, rubbed it, and placed it on his bed. Instead of the genie appearing, he saw a strange woman inside.

Marcus Bruce

"Hey!" he said excitedly, "get out of my crystal ball!" The
woman held up an unknown telephone number and pointed to it.
"I said get out!" Jimmy warned. But the woman kept pointing to
the phone number. "Wait a minute!" said Jimmy, he then went to
get a pencil. He wrote down every number and tried rubbing the
crystal ball once more. The woman appeared again and was still
pointing to the phone number. Jimmy held up his piece of paper
and showed it to the strange lady.

"See," he said. I've already got it!"

She nodded as if she understood and faded away. For the
third time he rubbed the crystal ball, the green smoke curled
and swirled inside. The room was full of a greenish smoke and
the genie, once large and powerful, was much smaller than
Jimmy had ever seen. His turban looked much larger and so did
everything else he wore.

"What the heck happened to you?" asked Jimmy.

"I don't know?" asked the genie, in a voice that reminded
Jimmy of some type of small chipmunk. Jimmy thought it comical,
he wanted to laugh, but unless he found out what was happening,
he knew that his life would suddenly change, and life would go
back to being as dull and boring as before. "I don't believe
this," he said. "What do we do now?"

"What is your wish oh mighty master?" asked the small genie,
in that weirdly high and wavering voice.

"You mean you can still grant me wishes?" asked Jimmy,
surprised.

"I don't know, but it's worth a try!" said the genie.

"OK," said Jimmy. Then he had a terrible thought. What if
the genie had only half his powers, the 'Fire Speed Deamon',
might be the size of a small ant. He imagined playing with a
toy the size of an ant.

The Amazing Adventures of Jimmy Jumpferjoy

"Wait a minute, hold it!" said Jimmy. "This is a big joke, forget it."

"Please let me try master!" said the genie seriously.

"Well, all right," said Jimmy. "You get three tries then back into the crystal ball, OK?"

The tiny genie put out his little arms and teeny-weeny sparks of magic and smoke flew out from his delicate finger tips. Nothing at all appeared. "Second try," said Jimmy. The small genie held out his puny arms again and sparks flew in every direction.

Suddenly the genie spoke. "You forgot to tell me what you wanted. I'm not a mind reader!"

"Oh . . . sorry . . ." said Jimmy holding his head with both hands.

"I want a 'Fire Speed Daemon!! It's a toy car. The genie stretched out his little arms and the magic sparks flew.

Before he could open his mouth and shout stop, Jimmy's bed had hot rod wheels, and the covers looked exactly like the shell of the 'Fire Speed Deamon' car.

"Let me try again master," pleaded the genie in his chipmunk sounding voice.

"Forget it!" said Jimmy, "Take it back." The genie reversed the spell and the bed was returned to normal. "I think I'd better call that lady," Jimmy said. "You'd better go back into the crystal ball." When the genie vanished, Jimmy dialed the phone number and a woman's voice answered.

"Hello," said a recorded message, "this is Fran. I do fortune telling at my home. I also make house calls. Stay on the line if you would like to speak to me in person." Jimmy stayed on the line and waited. Soon Fran answered.

"Who is it?" she asked cheerfully.

Marcus Bruce

"Well, my name is Jimmy jumpferjoy." Jimmy said.

"Yes, how may I help you?" Fran asked.

"Um, you were in my crystal ball."

"Oh, my, it's you!" said Fran. "You're in mine too!"

"I am?" asked Jimmy in confusion.

"Yes, let me give you my home address and we'll discuss it over tea."

"Right," said Jimmy.

The woman gave directions to her home. Jimmy flew there in a hurry on his magic carpet, and arrived there safe and sound. All of the windows had many thousands of glass beads hanging upon them. As he peered through the beaded curtain, he could see the living room window. The room was strangely lit with a thousand candles of different shapes colors and sizes.

"Come in!' she said. "Please tell me what's going on!"

"Don't ask me," Jimmy said. "I thought you knew!"

"All I know," said the woman "is that every time I try to tell someone's fortune, your face appears inside my crystal ball. For instance, I told one nice woman she would meet a very rich, tall, dark stranger, and guess whose face showed up in the crystal? The woman called me a fake and walked out fuming. Don't get me wrong. I like little boys. But not in my crystal."

"Well, I don't know. I think my problem is worse than yours," said Jimmy.

"Hardly," said Fran the fortune teller as she poured Jimmy a cup of herbal tea. "I've lost a job. If you keep showing up, I may never work again."

"Sorry," said Jimmy. "I bet I can figure it out. I'll give it some thought. As a matter of fact I'll sleep on it. That always seems to work." They drank their tea and Fran saw in the tea leaves a long journey for Jimmy.

"Well, OK," said Fran, "sleep on it. Please call me if you can figure it out, you have my number."

Jimmy hopped back on his magic carpet and went back home. He took off his shoes and watched television. Later that evening his father came home after a full day of job hunting.

"Hi Dad, find any good jobs yet?"

"No son I didn't. All they have for me are those junk jobs and I will not stand for that," his father exclaimed.

"But Dad," said Jimmy as he approached his father, "Mom was crying today. She said she didn't want to be poor any more."

"I'm sorry Jimmy, there just aren't any good jobs around any more."

"I know you're doing your best Dad," said Jimmy, "you'll make it." He patted his father on the back, turned and went to his room.

"Boy, oh boy," he said to himself. "I sure am tired, but I hardly did anything at all today." He curled up on top of his covers and fell fast asleep, before he could even take his play clothes off.

"Well well well," said a familiar voice, "if it isn't Mr. Jumpferjoy."

"Who else?" asked Jimmy.

"What do you want to do today?" said Jilly.

"Well, I've got a bad problem," he said with a big frown.

"What kind of problem?" asked Jilly.

"The kind of problem that gets on my nerves," he said. "My genie is loosing his powers or something, and a lady fortune teller keeps appearing in my crystal ball."

"Hey, that is a problem, isn't it?" said Jilly. "With that kind of magical crisis, I might end up never seeing you again."

"I don't know," said Jimmy. "Maybe we could see the
wonderful wise wizards again because I need an answer fast."

"Let's get going," said Jilly.

They went down the steep steps and Jilly placed her hand on
the door knocker. One friendly wizard opened the door while two
others bid them welcome.

"What is your question?" asked one of the wizards.

"Well, I just want to know what's been happening to my
genie."

The wizard placed his thin fingers over Jimmy's small
forehead. And just as before an image appeared on the Scanner
Screen: a bright pattern of stars. The image shifted and there
appeared Fran the fortune teller's sad face staring blankly
ahead, with Jimmy's face appearing in her crystal ball and her
face appearing in his. Once again the image changed. Now it
showed the genie in his present small state. He looked even
smaller than before, then the pattern arranged itself into a
blanket of stars in the night sky again.

"There's mischief in the heavens, my friend," began the
wizard. "The stars have taken a position that affects no one
else but those that play with real magic. That means you and
the woman will have to make a special journey to a lost island.
There, you will pick up a clear liquid that will stop the magic
from working against you. Miracle Fluid, it is called."

"There are certain rules you must follow. If you don't do
exactly as I tell you, the Miracle Fluid will not work. Listen
closely: Firstly, you must travel to the island by the sea.
Secondly, you and the woman must travel alone. Thirdly, you
must not bring the crystal balls with you. Fourthly, only one
of you can enter the special passageway where the Miracle Fluid

is hidden. There you have it. Good-bye." The wizard bowed and
turned and walked away.

"Um, thanks . . ." said Jimmy feeling confused and troubled.

"Yes, thanks," said Jilly cheerfully, waving goodbye.

The wizard looked at Jilly and gave her a small wink as he
closed the door.

The early morning sunshine woke Jimmy. He quickly called
Fran and told her about his visit to the wise wizards. He
explained what they must do and how they must go about it.

"There are certain rules we must follow if we want the
crystal balls to work. We're going to have to journey to an
island with the Miracle Fluid.

"I like to travel," said Fran. "I'll pick up tickets for an
ocean liner!"

"No way!" said Jimmy. "One of the rules states that we can't
be with other people; just us two. The Miracle Fluid will not
work unless we follow the rules exactly."

"Well you'd better explain the rules to me, 'cause I'm
getting just a little confused," she said. Once again, but
slowly, Jimmy told Fran all that the wise wizards had told him
about the stars and their position. Being familiar with reading
the stars, Fran looked at her star chart and told Jimmy that
he was every bit correct. They finished their conversation and
hung up the phone. Jimmy sat down to watch morning cartoons
while Fran made the arrangements she needed to take a long
trip. She said good-by to some dear friends, and asked the
neighbor to water her plants and feed her many cats. She then
met Jimmy at the park and they drove to the lumber yard. They
brought many planks of wood, some tar and many yards of cloth.
They spent the afternoon in Fran's back yard with their lumber
and constructed a strong sturdy raft. Tar was lathered thickly

Marcus Bruce

on the bottom, to keep it from leaking. A special compartment was made for storing food and water in the middle of the raft. The storage compartment could also be used to sleep on at night, or as a table. They completed the raft in three long days. On the last day, Fran went to the store and bought enough food for an entire month. "With the hungry little stomach I have, I hope this food will last," Fran observed under her breath.

Late in the afternoon, Joey called Jimmy on the phone.

"How are you doing?" he said.

"Fine," said Jimmy, "why?"

"My camp is letting us bring a friend up for a month," said Joey. "Of course I thought of you! What do you think of that?"

"Well, to tell you the truth, Joey, I'm kind of busy right now, but thanks for asking."

"That's OK, I'll ask somebody else. It's just that I wanted you to come. I thought I'd ask my best friend first, crazy!" said Joey laughing. Jimmy smiled as he hung up the phone. A great plan came to him suddenly. He could tell his parents that he was going with Joey to his Summer Camp. Now all he had to do was have them say it was all right to go. Crossing his fingers, he ran up to his mother with a big smile on his face.

"Mom, please say I can go to Joey's Summer Camp!"

"How long is it?" Jimmy's Mom asked curiously.

"He got me invited for a whole month! I'm really 'gonna have fun this Summer, right Mom?"

"A month is much too long!" said her mother sternly. "How much is it going to cost?"

"Free!" Jimmy beamed. "And I've never been to camp before. Please Mom, Please?"

The Amazing Adventures of Jimmy Jumpferjoy

"Free?" his Mom asked. "For a whole month? That's much much too long."

"Please Mom!" Jimmy said excitedly.

"I don't think so!" said his Mother.

"I'll learn new things!" he said.

"No! Jimmy, I still say that's just too long for you to be away from home at your age."

"But Mom, you and Dad can have the whole house to yourselves. For a whole month!

"Well . . . maybe," his mother answered looking less worried.

"A whole month!" said Jimmy. "Please just this one time!"

"Oh, all right! You talked me into it. I'll talk to your father. But take care of yourself. We can't afford to have you in the hospital. Understand?"

"I'll take care of myself, I promise," said Jimmy, grinning from ear to ear. He may have been smiling on the outside, but inside he was jumping up and down wildly. Now he could go on the journey with Fran, and his parents wouldn't worry. They probably wouldn't even miss him, he hoped. "Thanks Mom. If there's anything you want me to do just ask," he said happily.

"Just mind me! Take care of yourself," she said.

Everything for the journey was now in place. Fran met Jimmy at her street corner. The raft was inside of a trailer behind her old rusty Ford pick-up. Fran drove the truck, the raft, and Jimmy to the ocean pier, and they began their journey.

"How do we find the island?" asked Fran.

"Don't worry," said Jimmy. "I have a special telescope. We will find it, that's a promise."

Jimmy had brought his Telescope of Wonder. He had no need for his magic carpet, because he had to travel by water. He was

not allowed to bring his crystal ball, and if he had brought
it, he didn't even know if the genie would be helpful. Soon
the cool ocean breeze flowed over the raft. After they had put
up the sail, they ate a small snack. The seas remained calm
for the moment. The sail became round and full with the steady
wind. For now all they had to do was wait. They leaned back
against the rudder and watched the sun set and the moon rise
above their heads. Its rays reflected off of the choppy water
to give the sea a glistening look. As the moon set and the sun
shone once more, they pondered their fate at the hands of the
moody green sea.

They traveled for many hours swaying up and down with the
motion of the waves. Days passed, weeks passed, and all the
while, Jimmy kept a careful watch through his Telescope of
Wonder.

"Where do we go now?" Fran asked somewhat nervously.

"Well," Jimmy said, with one eye on the telescope and the
other eye tightly closed. "We're about to pass a very large
ocean liner."

"Wow! That must be a very powerful telescope. "I don't see
any sign of an ocean liner.

"Don't worry," said Jimmy, taking the telescope from his
eye, "believe me, you will!" Two days later they came upon a
huge ocean liner. As they slowly approached it, only a mile or
two away, the ship made a loud popping sound. The ocean liner
was gone without a single trace.

"My, oh my!" screamed Fran covering her mouth. "Did you see
that? The whole ship disappeared."

"I saw it! But I still don't believe it!" said Jimmy.

"Well, I hope that doesn't happen to us!" said Fran shakily,
as her eyes looked from side to side.

"Me too!" said Jimmy. The two really didn't have to worry, for luck seemed to be on their side.

Jimmy held the telescope up to his eye saying, "Show me the island." In the telescope he saw small people, natives of the island who looked to be very friendly. "Show me the secret passageway!" he commanded. He saw many unusual things; a woman with a melting face, a party of clowns and quite a few horrible monsters. "Um Fran? Remember I told you the rules we had to follow?" he asked.

"Yeah, you told me weeks ago," she answered.

"Well, since only one of us can go in the secret passageway, how about if you do it?"

he said, pointing his finger at Fran.

"Ask me again when we get closer!" said Fran. She took a hand full of peanuts and stuffed them into her mouth.

Onward they went, talking, laughing, singing, until the Sun set on the shimmering water. Night came swiftly. Before long Jimmy Jumpferjoy was fast asleep. This was the first time in a very long time that he was not able to go to Jilly Applejelly's world. The genie's powers were getting weaker and weaker every day. Soon Jimmy's Carpet, berries, and telescope would either disappear completely, or they would become useless.

The morning sunrise was absolutely beautiful, but Jimmy never saw it. He was having the most fitful slumber he had ever had. When he finally woke up, he saw Fran grinning from ear to ear. It was not a pleasant sight, for Fran's mouth was very wide indeed.

"Good morning," she said smiling.

"What's so good about it?" said Jimmy grumbling.

"We made it! That's what's so good!" Fran's smile appeared to get even wider than was humanly possible.

Marcus Bruce

"What?" asked Jimmy, shaking his groggy head from side to side. He grabbed onto the mast and pulled himself upward. He smiled happily at the sight of the uncharted island.

"Great!" he said. "Another hour or two and we can put our feet on land again."

"You know it's a good thing we found this island today!" said Fran.

"Why?" asked Jimmy.

"Just look in the food box silly!" laughed Fran. "We ate too much." She pointed to the food supply locker. They had used up almost all of their supply. It looked to Jimmy as if they had just enough food for a day or two more. What luck!

"If we hadn't found this island today, tomorrow would have been time for fishing lessons, and I don't know how to fish!"

"Yeah, and we don't have any matches either. How does raw fish sound to you? Yuck!"

"Well," said Jimmy, "right now, I feel like going on a sea food diet!"

"You want to eat raw fish?" Fran asked surprised.

"No, anything I see, I eat!" laughed Jimmy loudly. They laughed and laughed until both their stomachs ached.

"Dry off," said Fran, shoving his arm. "your jokes are all wet!" There went another round of gut splitting laughter. It was good to be back in the mood for fun again.

"Hey, say it, don't spray it!" said Jimmy, wiping his face of tears while still laughing.

When they arrived, the natives greeted them warmly. They were very nice and made many strange gestures. They didn't speak the same language as Jimmy. They used their hands to communicate. They appeared ready to help Jimmy and Fran on their search.

The Amazing Adventures of Jimmy Jumpferjoy

"Where is the secret passageway?" Jimmy asked a man who looked very old and withered. 'He must be the chief' Jimmy thought. The chief nodded his head in agreement, then handed Jimmy a handful of sea shells.

"No, No!" Fran yelled, trying to make herself understood, "the passageway!" The chief smiled while nodding his head. He then picked a flower and gave it to her.

Jimmy whispered, "Show me the entrance to the secret passageway," to his Telescope of Wonder. Luckily it was still working, and it showed the entrance to the passageway and everything around it. Jimmy put the telescope to the chief's eye. The chief nodded again, trying to figure out just what his visitors wanted.

"Where is it?" said Jimmy, shrugging his shoulders and pointing around him. Suddenly the chief understood. He walked off to his left and his warriors followed. Fran and Jimmy followed closely as well. While walking, they passed roaring waterfalls, wide rivers and tall cliffs until they arrived at the cave entrance, on the side of one of the cliffs. To the side of the entrance, was a small driftwood sign with words burned into it saying: Beware, Things are not always as they seem to be!"

"Who goes?" asked Jimmy, "you or me?"

"We'll draw straws. The one with the shortest straw wins," said Fran.

"I hope I don't win!" said Jimmy. But as fate would have it, poor Jimmy had the short straw. He nodded his head heavily and sat down. "Somebody talk me out of this!" he said, as he slowly walked toward the entrance.

"Bye!" said Fran, "and good luck!"

Marcus Bruce

Jimmy waved a final wave and everyone waved back, then into the cave he went. At first he was in total darkness. Jimmy held his hands out in front ever so carefully. He slowly put one foot in front of the other.

"Why doesn't somebody tell me where I'm going?" he said to himself. Soon he saw a dim light coming around a corner in the cavern. "Anybody home?" he yelled loudly. His voice echoed again and again until it faded away.

As he turned the corner, he found himself suddenly back at his old looking house, just around noon time. The bright Sun was shining. "I'm dreaming," he said. The front door opened and there was his mother looking right at him.

"You come her right this minute, young man!"

"I think I'm in trouble!"

"You bet you're in trouble!" said his mother. Joey's mother told me you didn't go to his camp like you told me!"

"Well, said Jimmy, "I . . . Um . . . I mean . . . I was um . . ."

"Don't lie to me again Jimmy. I want the truth!" said his mother angrily.

"Well, I went to an island?" said Jimmy sounding as if he were asking instead of telling her.

"That does it!" she said. "You're going to jail!"

"What?" Jimmy looked at his mother in disbelief.

"You heard me!" said his mother. She picked up the phone and dialed the police station. A police car pulled up and two tall police officers hand cuffed Jimmy and took him to the jail house and threw him behind bars.

"What's going on?" said Jimmy. "What did I do?"

"Don't you dare try to escape!" said the police officers in harmony as they walked away. Jimmy reached out and touched the

jail cell wall. It was like touching a large soft sponge. He
tore a hole in the wall of sponge and quickly snuck away. He
made his way down the shadows of the street; then hid behind
a small brown car which was parked in the street. He watched
the two police cars wiz by him and smiled. The brown car that
he was hiding behind floated into the air. When Jimmy looked
up, he noticed a giant of a man holding the car in his hand.
The giant tossed the car over a large fluffy white cloud and
pointed at Jimmy.

"Where is it?" asked the ugly mean giant, gnashing his
gnarly yellow teeth.

"Where is what?" asked Jimmy.

"Where's my golden harp?"

Jimmy laughed and said, "Ha, you've got the wrong guy
mister!"

"Don't laugh at me, you little ant of a person!" said the
angry giant, reaching down to grab Jimmy.

The giant picked him up in the air and tossed him over a
cloud also. As poor Jimmy was falling to the earth, a huge hawk
grabbed him by the shoulders and carried him off to her nesting
place.

"Ouch, let me go!" he screamed, "or I'll tell my genie
on you!" When she came to the place she let him drop among
the eggs in her nest. The nest was very large. All the eggs
looked like mighty white boulders except for one large black
egg with a dark string sticking out of the top. Being very
curious, Jimmy climbed over the other eggs to get a closer
look at the unusual black egg. The dark string began to
burst into sparkling flames without reason. "That's a wick!"
exclaimed Jimmy, feeling very nervous. "Oh, no, it's a bomb!"
It certainly was a bomb. Before Jimmy could escape there was

an ear shattering explosion and Jimmy was right in the middle
of it. He closed his eyes shaking with fright. Feeling dazed,
confused, but not hurt, he found himself in an all white room.

"Looks like some kind of hospital," he told himself. "But is
it a hospital?"

"No mister boy, you are with us!" said a small robot. "We
need you for an important experiment."

"What kind of experiment?" Jimmy asked.

"Well, if you must know, we have to cut open your body and
see just how your heart beats," said the robot.

"No you don't! You'll have to catch me first!" With that
he jumped off of the bed and began to run. Instead of running
forward, his legs carried him backward. Running into the wall,
his body broke it like a thin sheet of glass. Behind the wall
was a large pool of water which he fell backwards into. He was
then lifted up into the air and out of the water. He found
himself on a diving board. He was more confused than ever.
Shaking his head, he said, "What the heck's going on here?"

"Oh, there you are!" said a very beautiful woman, with
sparkling diamonds surrounding her gracious neck. "Please get
off of the diving board and join me for lunch."

"OK," said Jimmy.

"How long have you been waiting?" she asked.

"I wasn't waiting. I don't even know how I got here."

"Well, it doesn't matter does it?" she stated, "as long as
you are here!"

She gracefully invited him into her house and took out all
kinds of fancy foods. After dishing up herself and Jimmy, she
began to eat.

"So," she said, "how long have you been named Jimmy?"

"Ever since I was a little baby," he answered.

"What was that nice fortune teller's name?" she asked politely.

"Fran," said Jimmy, while buttering his potatoes.

"When do you think your father is going to get a good job?" she asked, while cutting into a small piece of steak.

"I don't know," said Jimmy. "Why are you asking me so many questions?"

"When did I do that?"

"Right now."

"You mean the day after yesterday?" the woman asked.

"I guess so," said Jimmy.

The woman took a deep breath then began to sweat. Large droplets of water dripped from her smooth forehead. Then Jimmy noticed something very strange happening. Her whole face was beginning to melt.

"Why do you look so frightened?" she asked calmly. Jimmy didn't utter a word. Instead, he stood up and slowly went for the door. As he reached for the knob, the door swiftly opened. Standing before him were two men dressed all in black, with very dark sunglasses. Jimmy backed up slowly and the two took off their sunglasses. Their eyes in their heads glowed a bright yellow.

"We got you now!" they said at the same time.

"Oh, my, yipes!" screamed Jimmy. He spun around only to see the woman with the melting face. Suddenly a young boy about his height ran by the window which was in back of the woman. Jimmy took off after him. The boy rushed around the corner of the house but Jimmy soon caught up with him. He grabbed the kid by the shoulders and turned him around. The boy looked like an exact copy of himself and Jimmy was stunned.

"Who are you?" Jimmy asked.

Marcus Bruce

"Who am I, who are you?" asked the strange kid.

"My name is Jimmy Jumpferjoy." Jimmy answered.

"Mine is Jilly Applejelly!" said the kid.

"You're crazy!" said Jimmy.

"No I'm not, watch!" said the kid and he quickly turned into Jilly.

"Oh my Garbo!" said Jimmy, and he let go of the kid. The false Jilly, grabbed Jimmy's hands and said, "Hurry up Jimmy, there are so many things I've got to show you." Jimmy jerked his hands away, turned around, and ran smack into a mirror. He was frightened at first, then realized it was his own image in the mirror.

"ha ha ha, he he he," laughed Jimmy, with a dumb expression, "I scared myself!" Suddenly, without warning, an orange and very ugly hand came out of the mirror, grabbed Jimmy by the throat and pulled him inside.

The orange hands belonged to a large, very ugly bluish monster with large round warts all over his face. The wild creature shoved Jimmy into a small river. But instead of sinking to the bottom, he floated on the water like vegetable oil. Jimmy shook his head and stood up and said, "I'm walking on top of the water, I don't believe this!" Finding it to be unusual, but fun, he began to jump up and down, trying to break the skin of the water. When he found he could not, he started to dance around and around, laughing all the while.

"Hey kid!" said a voice in the woods close by, "get off of the water!" The voice frightened Jimmy He was looked around cautiously then scurried off the edge of the river and pulled himself up. One short clown with a red and blue colored face, came from behind a tall tree and began to chuckle.

The Amazing Adventures of Jimmy Jumpferjoy

"Ha ha ha, I fooled you!" he said as he pointed his finger at Jimmy. As Jimmy walked past the happy clown, another clown came from behind another tree.

"Ha ha ha, fooled you!" said the other clown.

"That's right, fooled you," said the first clown.

"Cut it out!" demanded Jimmy, feeling embarrassed. As he walked further, he saw funny looking clowns coming from behind every tree. They were all laughing and pointing their fingers. "I said, cut it out!" yelled Jimmy. The clowns mocked him loudly.

"Cut it out!" they said, while laughing and pointing their fingers.

"For the last time, I said cut it out!" Jimmy yelled, boiling with anger. The clowns, one million in all, suddenly vanished. Their laughter faded gradually long after they were gone.

"Great!" he exclaimed, "they're all gone! This place is driving me crazy."

The very next thing he knew, he was shoved into an old looking black car. A cross-eyed man wearing a black derby spoke to him saying, "Hop in." Feeling suddenly rescued, Jimmy sat back in the car, safe at last.

"I'll drive you crazy!" screamed the man, blinking his crossed eyes. Suddenly Jimmy was flying wildly through the woods, holding on for dear life. He quickly jumped out of the car and rolled on the ground. As he dusted himself off, he noticed a large door standing alone, not more than four or five feet away. 'To the outside world' the sign read. Jimmy was glad to finally see there was a way out. He opened the door and standing just as he had left them was Fran. The natives looked upon him, mildly amused. Jimmy took a deep breath, then relaxed.

"Free at last!" he said cheerfully.

"Where's the miracle fluid?" asked Fran.

"Well, to tell you the truth, I didn't get it," Jimmy said wiping his forehead. "Let me tell you what happened.

"Isn't that the reason why we came on this journey?" snapped Fran, "For the miracle fluid?"

"I'm just glad to get out of that weird place!" answered Jimmy.

"The fluid!" said Fran gritting her teeth in disgust. "Where is the miracle fluid?"

"Don't get so excited," said Jimmy calmly.

"We just wasted our time!" said Fran angrily. "We left our homes to come to this lost island and you tell me you don't have the miracle fluid?"

"Calm down," said Jimmy, "just cool out!" Fran's face began to wrinkle up, like a dried prune, the natives simply frowned.

"Wait a minute!" said Jimmy. as they slowly surrounded him. "Hold it!" he said while trying to back away.

It wasn't hard to notice that Fran's face was turning a light purple and her gypsy clothes had turned a gruesome black. Her nose began to grow longer and everything about her resembled a fairy tale witch.

"Tie him up and throw him off the tallest cliff!" she commanded.

The natives brought thick vines from the forest and tied him up.

"Wait! I'll go back. I'll get the miracle fluid!" cried Jimmy.

The Amazing Adventures of Jimmy Jumpferjoy

"Much too late for that," said Fran, "much too late!" The
natives carried Jimmy to the top of the cliffs and tossed him
off.

Once again he was falling through the air. This time
however, an ugly dragon flew near and swallowed him up. He slid
down the inside of the dragon, deep into its stomach. Jimmy
sat alone inside the moist, slippery stomach, and all he could
think of was Jilly Applejelly.

"I wish she were here." He said to himself. "Things would be
much easier."

Appearing in front of him she said, "You want to get out
Jimmy?" He smiled and nodded his head. "There's the door," she
said, pointing to nothing but the skin on the inside of the
dragon.

"I don't see anything," said Jimmy.

"Look there," said Jilly, and a door magically appeared
where she pointed. She untied him and he opened the door.

"Come on Jilly," he said.

"You can go, but I'm staying," she said nervously.

"I'm going," said Jimmy. He closed the door behind him and
tripped over a dead log which was in front of him. He was free
falling in empty space, spinning around and around. "If I fall
just once more!" he said. "I think I'm going to be sick."

He fell through a soft roof and bounced on top of a smooth
bed. "Something tells me I didn't even leave this place," he
said to himself as he walked off the bed. He went into the
bathroom and saw a clear plastic cup filled with water on the
sink. "I need a drink," he said. "I'm thirsty." Putting the cup
to his lips he started to drink.

"This is it!" said a soft woman's voice inside his mind.

Marcus Bruce

He stopped, looked at the glass and suddenly realized that
the miracle fluid was in his hands. "Oh my Garbo!" he said,
filled with excitement. I have the miracle fluid."

"Without warning, the bathroom door slammed shut. This made
Jimmy Jumpferjoy slightly nervous. He almost dropped the cup.
He opened the bathroom door, and once again, standing before
him, stood Fran and the natives, just as he had left them.

"Did you get it?" asked Fran.

"Oh, no, not again!" said Jimmy.

"The fluid!" said Fran. "Did you get the fluid?"

Jimmy held up the cup. "I have it! I have it!" he yelled.

"Good," said Fran. They wrapped the cup in plastic wrapping
material and again in aluminum foil. They placed it into a
plastic food container. "I hope it doesn't evaporate," said
Fran.

"It better not!" said Jimmy.

They waved to the friendly natives of the island as they set
sail once more on their sturdy raft, and made for their long
journey across the sea. Jimmy used his Telescope of Wonder to
guide the way. At least twice, they survived stormy weather.
Before they had left the island, the people had gathered stores
of fruits, nuts and plants to last the entire trip home.

They kept active, playing games, singing songs and telling
stories. The only problem they encountered was a flock of
unkind seagulls that let them have it right on the top of their
heads.

Many days passed by. After a few weeks a sudden boredom set
in. Before long though, they were finally back where they had
started. Feeling very tired and smelling pretty bad, they got
out of the raft.

The Amazing Adventures of Jimmy Jumpferjoy

"Well Jim, you make a good partner!" said Fran proudly.
"Don't be a stranger!"

"Maybe when your crystal ball is working again, I'll let you
tell me my future," said Jimmy.

"Right," said Fran as she patted Jimmy on the back. They
laughed once more, long and hard and split the Miracle Fluid
into two separate cups. They said their good-byes, and went
their separate ways, somewhat sadly.

Jimmy felt a great relief when he greeted his Mother. "Did
you have fun at Joey's summer camp?" she asked him.

He crossed his fingers saying, "Mom, I had so much fun. I
almost didn't want to leave."

"All right!" she smiled as her young son headed off to play
in his room.

"This had better work," he whispered, sitting on his bed. He
took out his crystal ball and sprinkled some Miracle Fluid on
it. Then he stretched out his shirt and rubbed the crystal dry.
As he rubbed, once more his genie appeared, just as big and
jolly green as ever. "Good, you're better now. How about that
'Fire Speed Daemon' you promised me," said Jimmy.

"Yes, oh mighty master!" said the large and powerful genie,
in a very deep voice. He pointed his large finger with sparks
of magic flying in every direction. In Jimmy's hand appeared
the "Fire Speed Daemon', toy racing car.

"Oh, um, Genie," Jimmy said, "just one more thing. Could I
have magical powers like yours for just one day?"

The genie rolled his head back and laughed. "ha ha ha, I've
been waiting for this wish for a long time!"

"Well, can I?" asked Jimmy.

Marcus Bruce

The genie, with a smile on his large face, placed his enormous finger on Jimmy's small head and said. "There master, it is done."

"Great!" said Jimmy, "that's all for now." The genie went back into the crystal ball, and Jimmy went right to sleep.

The next day he woke up bright and early. After washing up, he wrote up signs to put up all over Artsville. Signs promoting his very own magic show.

By the afternoon, several people began to gather outside of the front of Jimmy's house. "Good afternoon ladies and gentlemen." Jimmy said with a flourish. "Welcome to Jimmy Jumpferjoy's Magic Show. For my first trick I'll need a lovely assistant." With the snap of his fingers, Jilly Applejelly appeared. Everyone clapped and whistled. "Most magicians need a place to work behind, so do I. That's why I need a magic table." Again, he snapped his fingers and a table appeared. "I'll need a top hat, a magic wand, and a bunny rabbit too," he said. Snapping his fingers they all appeared. The people went wild clapping and cheering. The dogs barked and babies cried. "With my magic wand's help, I'll pull an elephant from my hat."

"Then why am I here?" inquired the rabbit.

"I don't know," said Jimmy, "I guess you can go!" The fingers snapped, and with a puff of smoke, the rabbit was gone. The people laughed heartily.

One kid yelled out, "He can't pull an elephant out of a hat!"

"I can and I will!" said Jimmy dramatically. "And now, to your total amazement, watch!" he waved his magic wand over the top hat and the loud sound of an elephant was heard. "There you have it ladies and gentlemen, an elephant!"

The Amazing Adventures of Jimmy Jumpferjoy

"Fake!" yelled a kid from the audience. "That's a tape recorder." Jimmy reached into the top hat and pulled out an elephant's trunk.

"That's a gag from a joke shop!" yelled the kid.

"Watch carefully ladies and gentlemen! Don't let your eyes leave your face!" As Jimmy waved his magic wand over the top hat, a blinding flash of light made everyone close their eyes. A thick cloud of smoke cleared, and Jimmy and Jilly were sitting on top of a gigantic elephant! "Come here!' he said to the kid. "Put your hands on this animal and tell me it's a fake." Everyone in the crowd roared with laughter, making the kid grin foolishly.

Jimmy performed one amazing trick after another to a pleasant crowd until he was too exhausted to do more.

"In conclusion," he said, "after the show there will be free food and drink for everyone!" The people looked about at a barren street. "Just because you don't see it, doesn't mean it's not there," he said, waving his magic wand. "Look again!" Suddenly there were refreshment tents on the sidewalk, and the people applauded.

"Well ladies and gentlemen, that's the show for today. I hope you enjoyed it," he said, smiling meekly. The happy crowd clapped and whistled. They gave Jimmy a standing ovation that lasted for fifteen minutes. As the crowd cheered him on, he was overwhelmed with a great feeling of happiness. It was like nothing he had ever experienced before. With a sparkling gleam in his eyes, he bowed for the third and final time, and pointed to his assistant; the lovely Jilly Applejelly. She bowed once or twice herself, with the same delighted gleam in her eyes. That was the end of Jimmy's first magic show; but not the end of the magic, not at all.

Marcus Bruce